Bolan dropped his duffel bag into the cargo area

He wasted no time getting to the landing gear and taking a look outside. The small army surrounding the aircraft was focused on the chaos above. The soldier took advantage of their distraction and slipped out next to the wheel, with Smith hot on his heels.

"Now what?" Smith asked, peering out from their meager cover.

"Now we fight our way out," Bolan replied, "unless you have a better idea."

"None whatsoever. But we're a little outmanned, wouldn't you say?" the agent asked, pulling his gun.

The Executioner shrugged. "Just be ready on my go."

MACK BOLAN ®
The Executioner

The Executioner

Don Pendleton's®

EXTRACTION

A GOLD EAGLE BOOK FROM

WORLDWIDE®

TORONTO • NEW YORK • LONDON
AMSTERDAM • PARIS • SYDNEY • HAMBURG
STOCKHOLM • ATHENS • TOKYO • MILAN
MADRID • WARSAW • BUDAPEST • AUCKLAND

Recycling programs
for this product may
not exist in your area.

First edition July 2013

ISBN-13: 978-0-373-64416-2

Special thanks and acknowledgment to
Dylan Garrett for his contribution to this work.

EXTRACTION

Printed in U.S.A.

He that has eyes to see and ears to hear may convince himself that no mortal can keep a secret. If his lips are silent, he chatters with his fingertips; betrayal oozes out of him at every pore.

—Sigmund Freud,
1856–1939

Secrets are tricky things. Tell the wrong person an idle bit of gossip and your life's on the line. The golden truth is that dead men tell no tales.

—Mack Bolan

THE
MACK BOLAN
LEGEND

Nothing less than a war could have fashioned the destiny of the man called Mack Bolan. Bolan earned the Executioner title in the jungle hell of Vietnam.

But this soldier also wore another name—Sergeant Mercy. He was so tagged because of the compassion he showed to wounded comrades-in-arms and Vietnamese civilians.

Mack Bolan's second tour of duty ended prematurely when he was given emergency leave to return home and bury his family, victims of the Mob. Then he declared a one-man war against the Mafia.

He confronted the Families head-on from coast to coast, and soon a hope of victory began to appear. But Bolan had broken society's every rule. That same society started gunning for this elusive warrior—to no avail.

So Bolan was offered amnesty to work within the system against terrorism. This time, as an employee of Uncle Sam, Bolan became Colonel John Phoenix. With a command center at Stony Man Farm in Virginia, he and his new allies—Able Team and Phoenix Force—waged relentless war on a new adversary: the KGB.

But when his one true love, April Rose, died at the hands of the Soviet terror machine, Bolan severed all ties with Establishment authority.

Now, after a lengthy lone-wolf struggle and much soul-searching, the Executioner has agreed to enter an "arm's-length" alliance with his government once more, reserving the right to pursue personal missions in his Everlasting War.

1

Secret Service Agent Peter Cristoff sat in his rental car, enjoying a few last moments of tepid air conditioning and watching the chaotic mess outside the Marriott Hotel and Resort. The parking lot was teeming with cars as Secretary of State Arlen Foster prepared to leave Washington. Some were the vehicles of his staff members; some were police or Secret Service; a few were probably customers of the Marriott wondering what was going on.

Cristoff knew that any rank-amateur assassin could get through here as just another face in the crowd. That it took so many people to go along on a political junket and so many more just to get the man out the door was possible evidence that Foster was either incompetent or full of himself. Cristoff suspected both, but he'd never met the man.

Or maybe that's just the way it is with all politicians, he thought. Probably explains the deficit.

Ignoring the heat, Cristoff ran his index finger over the standard-issue 9 mm Beretta that sat in his lap and watched the airplane traffic circling for a landing at Dulles International Airport. His Glock was tucked at the small of his back and hidden by his sports coat. One of the two weapons he carried would be the one to kill a man he'd trained, a man he'd respected. But now Diego Gonzales was corrupt, willing to betray his nation for the promise of a payday. It didn't matter that Cristoff's employer was the one offering it.

What mattered was that he did what he'd been hired to do. After that, Gonzalez would be a liability to be removed from the equation. Still, Cristoff couldn't deny the worm of anxiety that crept through him at the thought of taking on Diego.

Well trained, Diego was a compact man with the kind of wiry muscles that meant he was both stronger than he looked and faster than he had any right to be. A skilled martial artist, he could fight with his hands and feet, and had qualified as an expert with his handgun. No, Diego wouldn't make it easy, but if "easy" was in his plans, Cristoff wouldn't be involved in a plot to kidnap the Secretary of State.

Some people were motivated by money, others by power, but Cristoff wanted glory. He'd dreamed of it from the time he'd first gotten into law enforcement. He wanted to be a hero and each idiotic criminal or boring protection detail made him want it more. His plan—the part his employer didn't know about—involved saving Foster at the last minute, ensuring that he would be a genuine American hero. He'd be offered his choice of assignments, and he already knew he'd move straight to guarding the President himself.

Still, for this trip, he'd maneuvered into the coveted role of lead agent. The best of the best and the one they sent when not just any field agent would do. There was only one lead on each mission, and no one was more dangerous or capable. At the least, it showed that his superiors held some respect for him. The Secretary of State wasn't a nobody.

Cristoff also felt a certain amount of sorrow. It wasn't difficult to picture Diego lying dead on the plane with a bullet wound in his chest, but he'd made his choices. Diego was willing to betray his country for money, but if he'd take Cristoff's money, it was only a matter of time until someone else came along and bought him again. That could end badly for Cristoff, so Diego had to die. There was no way that Cristoff would let the Secretary of State come to any harm on his watch. And no matter what he pictured, the reality was that Diego was very good and would likely be ready for a double cross. His own training and mission paranoia would tell him to expect it.

Traffic finally slowed and he decided it was time for him to join the group. He holstered the Beretta beneath his shoulder, double-checked that he had his credentials and stepped out of the car into the Washington, D.C., heat. There was something oppressive about the atmosphere in this city almost any time of the year. It wasn't just the weather, he believed. It was the hundreds, perhaps thousands, of politically driven egos all crammed into one space; it was a wonder that the city didn't spontaneously combust. Even in the dead of winter, D.C. felt like a hungry hell-beast waiting in the dark.

Cristoff crossed the parking lot and entered the hotel, moving nimbly through the crowded lobby and finding the elevators. At the door to the VIP elevator, a large Secret Service agent stopped him with an upraised hand until he flashed his ID. Giving Cristoff a grin, the agent stepped aside and pushed the button. When the doors slid open, Cristoff stepped inside, but just as they started to close a hand slipped in, blocking them.

"Hold that a second, would you?" a familiar voice said.

He stepped back to make room as the doors opened once more and Diego got on. Cristoff's heart picked up speed, but he schooled his features and gave no outward sign of knowing the other agent. The doors closed and both of them faced forward, knowing that the elevator cameras might be examined later for almost anything. Knowing they'd only have a minute alone, he nodded, indicating that it was safe to talk.

"Everything is a go?" Diego asked, his voice barely above a whisper.

"We're all set," he said. "No changes."

"And you…you're sure of this path?"

"There's no going back for either of us, Diego," Cristoff said. "When it's over, we'll be in charge of our own army and living like kings far away from the joys of the Secret Service."

The elevator doors opened and two more agents were waiting to check their identification. Once they were cleared, one agent escorted them to the Secretary of State's room. The secretary stood in the middle of a swarm of attendants and staffers as Cristoff and Diego strode forward.

This part of the plan was relatively simple and called for him to take the lead. He would be less intimidating than Diego.

"Secretary of State Foster," Cristoff said as he reached Foster's side.

"Yes?" he asked.

"We're the new agents you've been expecting," he said. "I'm going to be in charge of your personal security on this trip. Peter Cristoff." He offered his hand, which the secretary took in a firm grip and shook briefly and politely.

He nodded. "Yes, of course. Thank you for coming, though I admit I was a little surprised when I heard about the last minute change. I know my own security detail, and I don't particularly like being told that I have to do something without an explanation. I don't suppose either of you would care to explain what's going on?"

Cristoff shrugged. "We simply have particular knowledge of that part of the world, Mr. Secretary. Considering the current tensions in Madagascar and the many factions involved in the political climate, our superiors believed that it would be wise to send a couple of agents with specific expertise."

Foster gave them a hard stare for a moment, then turned to his assistant. "Pam, are we all set here?" he asked.

"Yes, sir," she said.

"Then let's get this show on the road." Foster gestured to the various staff members in the room. "Get them moving in the right direction."

Pam, a woman with dark brown hair and a voice loud enough to be easily heard over the various conversations in the room, started heading the people off in various directions, explaining what had to be done and where they were supposed to go.

"Are we ready?" Foster asked, turning back to Cristoff and Gonzalez.

"Absolutely, sir," Diego said. "Please come this way."

Diego moved out in front of the Secretary of State and Cristoff fell in directly behind him, escorting him down the hallway to the elevator. The assistant caught up quickly and engaged him with a variety of last-second topics and questions that he answered as they walked. Cristoff was relieved, because it kept the secretary from asking them any more questions. The conversation continued all the way to the vehicles waiting outside to take them to a private runway at Dulles.

Diego, Cristoff and the assistant got into one vehicle with the secretary; two more cars made up the small motorcade. Airport security cleared a path for them as they drove out to the runway. Other than the shuffle of papers as the Secretary of State reviewed notes, and the minute tapping sound of fingers on a smartphone as his assistant sent a text message, the short ride was quiet.

When the car stopped, Diego got out first, followed by Cristoff, the Secretary of State and Pam. The two other vehicles also came to a halt, and four additional Secret Service agents and four more staff members got out. Everyone else had stayed behind at the hotel or gone back to the office.

The plane was already warming up as they made their way to the steps and got onboard. After everyone was seated and settled, the flight took off for the long journey to Madagascar. Cristoff seated himself next to the Secretary of State—a place he didn't plan on relinquishing until he had Diego and the rest of the security detail dead and the plane secured.

About an hour into the flight, Foster set aside his papers and gave Cristoff a long, speculative look. "So what is it you aren't telling me?" he asked.

Cristoff returned his stare blandly. "I'm not sure what you mean, sir," he replied, keeping his voice neutral.

"Call me Arlen," he said. "And what I mean is that this is more Secret Service than I've ever had on any diplomatic mission, and I've been to some dangerous places. Madagascar may be a bit hot right now, but it's not terribly unstable, either. Six agents and a new lead at the last minute?" He shook his head. "That doesn't make sense, Agent Cristoff."

"I just do what I'm told, sir, and it's against protocol to refer to you by your first name. They tell me to go protect someone, and that's what I do. I served a year at the embassy there, so perhaps that's why they asked me to lead."

"A convenience, Agent Cristoff, and I suspect you know it. Are you going to share with me what's going on, or do I get to keep guessing?"

Cristoff considered the question carefully, trying to decide the best way to answer this man who was more perceptive than he'd anticipated. "Mr. Secretary, I'm sure that everything will be fine. Just stick close to me, and I'll make sure you get to where you need to go."

"Just you?" he asked. "What about your partner or the other four agents on this plane?"

"Unless there's a change, I have the pleasure of being your primary support right now," he said.

"Still not going to tell me what's going on, huh?"

"I'm not sure what else to say to reassure you, Mr. Secretary. It's my job to keep you safe, and I will."

Foster snorted in disbelief. "Young man, I've been in politics a long time and I listen to bullshit for a living. I can always tell when someone is holding back." He shrugged. "I'll let it go for now, but my patience only goes so far."

"I understand, sir." Cristoff turned away from the man's penetrating gaze to stare out the window. The man saw far too much for his own good, and if Cristoff wasn't careful, Foster would see right through him. At this point, that might be fatally dangerous to him or any number of other people on the plane. The entire plan revolved around Diego's help—and death—at critical times. If the secretary tried to play hero, it could go bad in a hurry.

The rest of the flight was quiet, with one brief stop in Paris for fuel. Even the meal service was subdued as Foster absorbed himself in his work and talking with his staff. One quick layover in Paris for fuel and the chance to stretch their legs caused little delay. Shortly after eating the secretary took a nap, which gave Cristoff the opportunity to work his way to where Diego was sitting three rows back.

"How's it going with the Secretary of State?" he said, keeping his voice pitched low enough that only Cristoff could hear him.

"Fine, though he's suspicious about the change in security," he said.

"Do you think it will be a problem?"

He shook his head. "Not really. What's he going to do?"

"Not a thing," Diego said. He glanced at his watch. "You should get back up there, try and get some rest. We've still got a ways to go."

"Too wired to sleep," Cristoff admitted.

Diego grinned. "I can think of a way to calm your nerves. That blonde flight attendant might be just the thing, but maybe this isn't the flight to join the Mile High Club."

"Very funny," he said, trying his best to not reveal that, in his mind, Diego was already dead and that talking to him was more than a little spooky.

"Just a thought," he said. "A man can't survive on work alone."

"It'll have to do for now," he said. The Secretary of State stirred slightly in his seat. "I've got to go."

"Try and rest, Cristoff," Gonzalez said. "We're good to go until we land."

"I'll try," he said, touching the other man once on the shoulder and then heading back to his seat. It was the best goodbye he would be able to manage. Once he sat down, and despite his earlier protest, he found that it was possible for him to doze, and eventually he drifted off.

2

The unconscious man sprawled across the rumpled bed was known as *El Varacco*—the Boar. Mack Bolan, aka the Executioner, thought of him by a different appellation, *El Cerdo Gordo*—the Fat Pig. Both names fit him well enough. Bolan checked the only door once more as the woman he'd hired to distract *El Varacco* finished putting on her clothes. In the mirror, the reflection showed the long, lean form of a woman in prime physical condition, but Bolan didn't have much time to admire the scenery. He had a job to do and the clock was ticking.

Reaching beneath the cluttered desk, Bolan—Matt Cooper these days, when he was on a mission—pulled the small Glock from its hiding place and slid it into the small of his partner's back. She tied back her long black hair in a simple ponytail, then put on her black leather trench coat. With the white silk blouse and the black denim jeans covering the tops of her boots, she felt about as prepared as she was going to be for the final phase of this mission and hoped she wouldn't falter under the pressure. Rosalita was as brave as she was beautiful and her thirst for vengeance was powerful. *El Varacco's* killing of her brother had created a fiery hate in her, and when Bolan needed a female accomplice, Hal Brognola from Stony Man Farm sent her his way.

The city of Ciudad Juarez, just across the border from El

Paso, was awash in drugs and crime. Despite the Mexican government sending troops and bolstering law enforcement, an alarming number of illegals were still crossing the border, and with them came an even more alarming amount of drugs, particularly cocaine, methamphetamines and heroin. Murders were as common as walking, and the last handful of honest citizens lived in fear. *El Cerdo Gordo* was responsible for a major portion of the drugs and the crime, and he'd enjoyed getting rich off people who wanted to immigrate to America, selling drugs, and killing soldiers and police to protect his own interests.

At Hal Brognola's request, Bolan had gone south to infiltrate *El Cerdo Gordo*'s organization and kill him. It was a temporary solution at best, but for a time it would stem the tide. This night was the culmination of almost three weeks of work that had mostly involved massaging *El Cerdo Gordo*'s ego and sending pretty women his way.

The Executioner looked at the unconscious, naked, fat man, whose most enduring personal qualities were a lack of hygiene and a tendency to consume too much of his own product, and grimaced. Fortunately, he'd been dumb enough to accept Bolan's offer of tequila straight from the bottle when Rosalita had gotten him to his room. After five minutes of clumsy kissing and flirting, he'd stripped out of his clothes and hit the bed, totally incapacitated. A few drops of a simple compound, sodium pentobarbital—a horse tranquilizer used for euthanasia—in the bottle of tequila had proved very effective in putting him into a deep sleep.

Removing a thin blade from his right boot, Bolan moved closer to his target. He glanced at Rosalita, silently offering her the chance to alter the outcome, but the determination to see it through was there in her eyes. He took a pillow and placed it over the drug lord's head, though he didn't expect him to stir, then immediately handed her the knife. Without comment, Rosalita slid the blade into the man's fat throat. The razor-sharp edge sliced through the skin as if it were paper and found his jugular. Pulling the blade free, she moved aside and let the blood flow into the heavy cotton of the pillow. In a few, brief moments, *El Cerdo Gordo* was so much dead meat.

She wiped the blade clean on the pillowcase, tossed a blanket over the dead man, then handed the knife back to Bolan. *"Adios, perra,"* she whispered, as the soldier put the blade back into his boot.

Now came the hard part, Bolan knew. Taking him out had been too easy; despite *El Cerdo Gordo*'s fierce reputation, he was the same as any other man when the blood rushed away from his brain in the direction of his crotch.

His main lieutenant, however, was a different story. Juan Ramirez was the man who really kept the operation running and the small compound safe. No one entered or left the courtyard without authorization, but Bolan could get around that. What he really needed to do was make sure Ramirez was dead so that the whole setup crumbled. And Ramirez wouldn't be so stupid as to accept an open bottle of tequila.

In fact, Bolan knew Ramirez had suspected him from the day he had shown up in the city. Most likely, Ramirez had allowed Bolan's access only to further Juan's own ambition. His room was on the ground floor. Rosalita picked up the low-crowned felt cowboy hat from the bedpost and put it on, then moved to the door. Opening it cautiously, she peered out as the hallway guard turned in her direction.

Rosalita stepped into the hall leaving the door open a crack. Bolan watched as she sashayed along the corridor, fully garnering the guard's attention.

"Que pasa?" the man said.

"Duerme," she whispered, putting a finger to her lips.

The guard grinned and nodded as she moved past him. *"Buenas noches,"* she said.

"Buenas noches, señorita," he replied, watching as she moved down the stairs.

The Executioner waited for them to turn their backs, then he moved across the hallway to the back staircase. He reached the bottom of the steps then silently slipped down the hallway to the room where Ramirez slept. The two guards who patrolled this floor had to have been walking near the back or the front of the main house, rather than here, which was good. It would make this easier if he didn't have to take them on or try to come up with a reason he was there in the first place.

Bolan tried the door, found it unlocked and opened it quietly.

What he expected was to find Ramirez sleeping. What he found was Ramirez sitting on his bed, wide-awake and obviously waiting for him.

"I've been expecting you," he said in Spanish.

Hiding his surprise, Bolan closed the door behind him. "Happy not to have disappointed you."

"¿Quién son usted, realmente?"

"Who am I?" Bolan said, reverting to English. "I'm your executioner."

"The angel of death," Ramirez whispered, moving off the bed. He pulled a heavy blade from a sheath on his hip.

"Many have tried to clip my wings, but I'm still here," Bolan replied, drawing his own knife, and moving closer with deceptive speed. Surprised, Ramirez backed away, waving the blade through the air in the sinuous pattern of an experienced knife fighter.

Bolan ducked low, sliding beneath his opponent's guard and left his weapon buried in Ramirez's thigh. Cursing, the man took a split second to pull it free and the blood began to spurt. Bolan had caught the femoral artery and Ramirez had only moments to finish the fight and get help. Bolan glided backward, trying to avoid being covered in blood, which would make it very difficult to escape unnoticed, let alone get on a plane home.

Ramirez's eyes widened in horror as he became aware of the situation. *"Diablo,"* he grated, lunging forward.

Bolan stepped gracefully to one side, avoiding the wide, swinging arc of the blade. Weakening, Ramirez stumbled and Bolan slipped behind him, pulled a garrote wire from his belt and whipped it around his neck.

Shoving a knee into Ramirez's back, the soldier used leverage to force him slowly to the floor. Ramirez thrashed and bucked beneath him, trying to use his greater weight and strength. Blood pumped from his thigh onto the floor, coating it in sticky crimson. Bolan tightened the wire around Ramirez's neck, completely cutting off his oxygen, and his nearly silent grunts of exertion slowed rapidly as his last vestiges of strength faded. It was over in less than a minute.

Ramirez shuddered one final time, then his bowels let go as death claimed him. Overall, it was a nasty bit of business, but Bolan had seen far worse. He left the garrote around his adversary's throat and picked up his knife from where the dead man had dropped it on the floor. Using one of the bedsheets, he wiped the blade clean and replaced it in his boot.

Moving to the door, Bolan paused to listen, and when he heard nothing, he stepped into the hallway, closing the door behind him. From the back of the building, he could hear the muffled laughter of the house guards. Bolan walked in speedy silence to the front of the structure, opened the main door and stepped into the courtyard. It was covered in shadows as clouds passed overhead.

Slipping toward the front gate, he saw that the guards were watching the street, not the courtyard itself. Still, if he could get through without leaving any more bodies behind, he would. There was no point in killing if it could be avoided. Many of these men were little more than barrio thugs who would work for anyone if it meant a decent day's pay and a meal. Few had any idea of the impact of their actions on the wider world.

A small door was set into the wall on one side of the gate and Bolan hid himself in the shadows. The door was locked with a sliding bolt from the interior and a heavy, keyed dead bolt. The bolt was out of the way quickly, but the lock would be another matter. Reaching into his coat, he removed a small leather case that held his picks and set to work in the cramped space, trying to be as quiet as possible.

He felt the first pins in the lock give at the same moment that he heard shouts from within the house. He tried to work faster, even as someone began ringing a loud bell. Overhead, he heard the guards shouting questions and two floodlights came on and began sweeping the courtyard.

"Shit," he muttered, even as the last pins released. Bolan twisted the dead bolt handle and opened the door as four guards ran into the courtyard from the house. More lights came on as the guards shouted in Spanish.

One of them, the man who'd been upstairs, began shouting and pointing in his direction.

He'd been spotted and he turned, pulling his Desert Eagle free even as he stepped into the open doorway. The modified weapon felt like an extension of his own arm as he laid down several rounds, forcing the guards to dive for cover even as they opened up with their own weapons.

Unfortunately, the guards overhead now knew Bolan's position, which meant that running out the door wasn't going to work. And they had machine guns.

Bullets whined and cracked against the adobe walls as the guards in the courtyard tried to get a shot in. Bolan quickly calculated what his options were and didn't like any of them in particular. An idea occurred to him, and he shouted, *"¡Me entrego! ¡No tire!"* telling them that he gave up and not to shoot.

One of the men called for him to drop his gun and kick it into the courtyard. *"No puedo. Me dañan. Ayúdeme, por favor,"* he replied, telling them he couldn't because he was injured and asking for help.

Stupid, he thought as they rose from their hiding places and began walking in his direction. He knelt in the shadows between the walls and the inset doorway, assuming a posture of injury, his weapon held close to his body.

The guards foolishly grouped up as they moved closer, all of them trying to see at once. He waited for them to get closer still and as the first one knelt, he moved with the blinding speed that was one of his hallmarks. The Desert Eagle came up and killed the kneeling man and two others before they had a chance to do more than register surprise on their faces.

Rolling backward, he continued to fire, even as the other guards forced themselves closer…and out the door, thus confusing the guards on the wall and making it impossible for them to shoot for fear of hitting their comrades. The last man fell dead in the dusty ground, and the soldier counted his blessings that the confusing swarm of bodies kept the guards from getting a clear shot.

The guards on the wall were still peering down at the chaotic scene when he placed a round into each one with smooth precision. They fell off the wall and into the courtyard below. Inside the compound, more shouts were starting as people and guards were waking up and trying to figure out what was going on. He needed to move quickly and climbed to his feet, then turned and sprinted into the night.

Bolan knew he'd have to stop somewhere and clean up, but a glance at his watch told him that he had plenty of time to do that, pick up his few personal items from the hotel where he'd taken a room, and still make his flight back to Dallas.

This hadn't been his most difficult mission by a long shot, but even the relatively easy ones were tiring. What he really wanted was to get home and have a good meal and a long soak. But until he was safely on the ground in the United States, what he needed to do was focus on getting away.

A mission wasn't a success unless you came back alive. And that was something he intended to do for a long, long time to come. In the darkness behind him, he could hear sirens as the police came to investigate all the shooting. Bolan could imagine what a short investigation that would be, and how many prayers of thanks would be offered that *El Varacco* was dead.

Sometimes, he thought, turning a corner and seeing the lights from his hotel ahead, even the simple missions provided good things for the people involved. He wasn't saving the world on this one, but he was making things a little better for the border and the people who lived there.

For Bolan, his life's work—whether it was a mission from Stony Man Farm or something he undertook on his own—was entirely about saving the people who needed saving and doing the jobs no one else could do.

He was the Executioner, and nobody did it better.

3

When the captain's voice came over the intercom, Cristoff almost jumped out of his seat.

"We're going to begin our descent to Antananarivo shortly, but there's a pretty violent thunderstorm going on down there. It may get just a tad bumpy coming in, so if everyone will kindly stay seated and buckled in, we should be on the ground in about a half hour."

He'd no sooner signed off than the first jolt of turbulence seemed to pick up the plane and then slam it back down into an air pocket lined with concrete. The whole plane shuddered.

"Jesus," Cristoff muttered as the plane was jostled around the suddenly violent skies.

"I guess he wasn't kidding when he said a little bumpy," Foster said, his blue eyes bright with interest.

"I'm thinking our pilot should get an award for understatement of the year. Of course, they never say, 'Hang on, everyone! We'll be lucky if we don't end up a fiery wreck when we hit the runway.'"

Foster stared at him, obviously not sharing his sense of humor. Cristoff looked out the window, catching sight of lightning flashing in the distance. It was far enough away from the plane that it didn't look to be an immediate threat, but that could change quickly. Either way, it was a pretty serious storm, at least at their current altitude.

Cristoff made a mental adjustment, trying to determine if the severe weather required an adjustment to his plan. Diego was several rows back, and as soon as they were on the ground, his job was to move to the rear of the plane and let Rija's forces on board through the rear exit. Cristoff's role was to keep the secretary pinned in the front of the plane, while letting the militia men in through the main entry. Of course, his real intention was to kill Diego the second he opened the rear hatch, which would alert the other agents on board. By then, the attacking militia would be clear to everyone, the pilot would take off—and he'd be a hero.

Cristoff stared out the window awhile longer, knowing that the downpour would make a perfect cover for the militia. The plan should still be good. Another bolt of lightning lit the sky, and the plane shuddered on a follow-up wave of thunder. Cristoff began thinking that he may not have to worry about killing Diego. God seemed determined to do it for him and take everyone else on the plane along with him.

"Listen, Mr. Secretary," he said. "I've got a bad feeling here. Call it gut instinct if you want. But when we get on the ground, I need you to do exactly what I say, okay?"

"You're going to have to give me more than that, young man," Foster snapped. "As it is, I'm tempted to report you to your superiors. All this skulking around. I have a right to know what's happening."

"Just do it, okay?" Cristoff gritted his teeth, his nerves strung tight. Typical, he thought. I get the guy who can't obey orders without asking questions.

Before he could answer, the pilot came back on and said, "Sorry for the rocky ride, folks. We're beginning our final descent now and should have you on the ground in just a couple of minutes."

He felt the plane complete a short half-circle, and then it began a sharp descent. In his mind, he reviewed what he would need to do one last time. There was little room for error. Cristoff risked a glance over his shoulder and Diego gave him a quick nod, already unbuckling his seat belt. He would have to move quickly or they'd be overrun before he could stop it.

A small stutter-step thrummed beneath his feet as the wheels touched down. "I still want to know what you're talking about," Foster said.

They were on the ground—safe for the moment—but the real danger was about to begin.

"I'm pretty sure you're about to find out," he whispered.

When the small plane came to a halt, Cristoff peered through the windows on the far side and could see at least three military-type jeeps rushing across the concrete. Seconds after the plane stopped, Cristoff saw Diego jump out of his seat and move toward the back. In the front, one of the flight attendants was blindly moving to open the front door, which shouldn't have been happening at all. Safety protocol required him to wait until the plane reached the terminal and stopped, but… Cristoff shook his head. The whole thing was about to come unraveled.

A couple staff members were already up and moving to the front of the plane, including one of the agents, which meant that Cristoff couldn't get to the out-of-place flight attendant in time.

"Stay here and stay down," he ordered Foster as he moved into the aisle. "Something's going on."

"What is it?" Foster asked, but Cristoff ignored him. As he moved toward the back of the plane, shots rang out from the front.

As he'd suspected, the flight attendant was a plant, which meant that…

He spun and moved in that direction, trying to keep himself between the advancing sounds, the Secretary of State and Diego all at once. Three of the Secret Service agents rushed toward the front of the plane and the first one died about two steps out of the main cabin area, cut almost in two by automatic weapons fire.

"Move away from the door!" he shouted, trying to keep people inside the plane where it was marginally safer.

Cristoff's words were lost in a hail of bullets as Rija's militia men stormed the front of the plane. The situation was going to get ugly in a hurry, and he repositioned himself, shoving the Secretary of State to the side.

"Get down on the floor, you damn fool," Cristoff snapped.

For once, the man didn't talk but just hit the deck, curling up between the seats.

The last remaining Secret Service agent, a big guy, moved past him toward the back of the plane, completely ignoring the threat from the front. Cristoff fired twice, at the men entering the plane, briefly slowing the surge with two corpses that the remaining soldiers would have to climb over.

He heard shots behind him and risked a quick glance to see that the other agent was holding his own. The rear doorway was smaller, so it made causing congestion easier. Outside, he heard Diego shouting orders, telling the men to get on the plane. Why would they be taking orders from Diego? he wondered, his thoughts wild. They don't even know him. Nothing was connecting the dots.

Three more men came through the doorway and there was nothing Cristoff could do to stop the one who turned and took out the pilot, copilot and another flight attendant with three quick bursts. Doing his best to ignore the screams from the staff members on the plane, he ducked behind a seat as the militiamen turned their attention on the passengers.

Several died before he had a chance to do more than risk a look and fire once, taking out the closest one with a round to the chest. At his feet, he could hear the Secretary of State's rapid breathing. Toward the front, he heard someone yell, *"The secretary. Get the secretary!"* None of this was going according to plan at all.

Behind him, several quick shots rang out, and he turned in time to see the last Secret Service agent go down in a heap, landing awkwardly in a row of seats. The whole thing was coming apart. He peered between the seatbacks, and when one of the militia soldiers risked a look around the corner of the cabin, Cristoff took him between the eyes. The soldier flipped over backward with an ugly, cutoff groan.

More soldiers were coming into the front of the plane, though, and it was only a matter of time.

At the rear of the plane, Diego was yelling, *"Cease fire!"* The few remaining people on the plane had screamed themselves silent. Cristoff kept his position, all but standing on top of the crouching Secretary of State, whose eyes were wide. He looked like he wanted to say something, but Cristoff shook his head sharply.

He could hear the sound of booted feet from both ends of the plane, and knew that the soldiers on board were inching closer to his position. There was no way he could take them all, and he briefly wondered how many had died this day, all so Rija could take on the government. It was all so stupid, and worse than that, Cristoff had obviously been betrayed—double-played by both Diego and Rija.

Cristoff peered through the seats in both directions. It looked like there were now at least four or five militiamen toward the front, with an additional three behind him. The angle was bad and it was hard to tell for certain. All he knew was that, short of a miracle, he was as good as dead.

"What's going on?" Foster hissed at his feet.

He spared a moment to glare at him as he pulled the Glock from behind his back and moved the Beretta to his left hand.

From the rear of the plane, he heard Diego remind everyone

not to shoot. "He's closer to the front," he said. "Everyone stay calm."

Cristoff eased his way out of his crouch and into the aisle. He kept one weapon pointed in either direction. "Tell them to back off, Diego!" he called.

"Hold it!" Rodriquez snapped. All the soldiers stopped moving, but they kept their guns aimed directly at Cristoff.

"Cristoff, come on," Diego said. "It's over. I knew you couldn't do it, not really, but it doesn't have to be this way. It's not too late for you to join up. It beats being dead."

Cristoff couldn't see Diego from where he was standing, which meant that taking him out at this point was almost impossible. "You're right, Diego," he said. "I can't do it. But no one else has to die. Rija's made his point. Take your men and go."

"It can't end here," he said. "You know that. He's going to make an excellent bit of leverage."

"Leverage?" Foster said from his position between the seats. "What the hell is going on?"

"It ends now," he called, ignoring the secretary. "I won't let you take him."

"Then you leave me no choice," Diego replied. "Kill him!"

"Shit," he said, even as the soldiers moved to fire. Diving back down beneath the seats, Cristoff opened up with both weapons, sticking the barrels between the seats.

The closest two soldiers in either direction went down and Cristoff adjusted his position slightly, moving toward the middle row of seats. As he did, he realized that for a split second, he'd exposed himself to a shot from behind.

Stupid! The thought raced across his mind in the milliseconds before he felt a burning pain slice across his temple and the fiery impact of a round taking him in the chest. It knocked him off his feet and his vision spun crazily for a second, as alternating darkness and sparkles of light flared in front of his eyes.

Cristoff knew he was dead, the Secretary of State captured.

He had failed. There would be no glory. The betrayer had been betrayed. He wouldn't be a hero. His vision cleared long enough for him to see Diego standing over him, prepared to shoot him again, should it prove necessary. It's not, he thought, taking a hitching breath filled with the copper taste of blood.

His last thought was that he should have taken Diego's suggestion to join the Mile High Club.

4

His cell phone rang at the same time as the alarm clock, and Bolan reached for both, silencing the one with a flick of his wrist. The ringtone for an incoming call from Stony Man Farm always got his attention, so he didn't bother to look at the number before he answered. "Striker," he said, his voice still gruff with sleep.

"And good morning to you, too, sunshine."

A brief chill of foreboding ran down Bolan's back. As the director for the Sensitive Operations Group based at Stony Man Farm, Hal Brognola wasn't the kind of man to use "sunshine" or any other words that sounded soft, cuddly or even particularly warm, so the greeting brought immediate suspicion.

There had been a time when Bolan ran the antiterrorist organization that answered only to the President of the United States, but that was long ago. Now Bolan kept the group at arm's length—working with them regularly, but free to pursue missions on his own, as well. Not that it mattered, but while Stony Man Farm could and often did take on problems that were either too dangerous for the regular agencies of government to handle—or too delicate to be handled through official channels—the extra remove suited Bolan's temperament and style. He didn't want to be answerable to anyone but himself. That was burden enough.

"Fair enough," he replied. "Good morning to you, Hal, and whoever else is listening in to our call."

"How did he… You were supposed to…"

The sputtering continued from the other end of the call as Bolan switched his own phone over to speaker and pulled on a pair of sweatpants. He moved silently to his own laptop, powered it up and logged in. Vaguely, he heard Hal say, "I told you he'd know."

"What would I know, Hal?" he asked, thinking that, at the moment, what he really wanted to know was how long it would take to get the coffee going. When a person spent enough time in the field, the small comforts like a coffeemaker were a wonderful thing.

"Matt," Brognola said, using one of Bolan's cover names, "I'm here with an…advocate from the office of the Secretary of the Interior. His name is Mr. Jacobs, and there's a priority situation that's come up that needs your special skills."

"I still don't see why we can't just send our man," Jacobs said. "I mean, I know that the President—"

Brognola cleared his throat sharply, and Bolan could easily imagine his dark stare as he glared Jacobs into a chair and silence.

"As I was about to say, and as Mr. Jacobs already knows, the President wants you on this thing."

"What's the situation, Hal?" Bolan asked.

"Early this morning, Secretary of State Arlen Foster was kidnapped in Madagascar."

"Was he on some sort of secret visit?" he asked. "What about his protection detail?"

"We're still finalizing the site intelligence," Brognola replied. "But the short answers are that, no, this was a planned diplomatic visit, and other than one missing agent, all the other members of his protection detail were killed."

Bolan was immediately suspicious about the missing agent.

It seemed most likely that he was involved—after all, it was their job to die rather than let their protectee come to harm. "Who's claiming responsibility?" he asked.

"A local militia group that wasn't even on our radar until all of this started up. They claim that they have him, and they're asking for the U.S. to give them weapons in exchange for his safe return. And we don't—"

"Negotiate with terrorists," all three men said in unison.

"From what we've learned so far, the current government isn't very popular, especially in the more rural areas of the island. They're asking that we keep this quiet and let them handle it. Obviously, it creates a problem if we send in troops of our own, because we'd have an even bigger diplomatic mess to deal with."

Bolan thought about the angles. "I smell a rat," he said. "A big one. Something isn't right about this."

"Agreed," Brognola said. "But that doesn't change the fact that they have Foster, and the President wants you to get him out."

"It's got to be quiet," Jacobs chimed in. "If it's not, then the Madagascar government will be forced to say that we took aggressive action—otherwise, it's going to look like they're not in control of their own damn country. And frankly, we don't need any of the possible PR problems a military action like this—let alone the loss of the secretary—would create in our own country."

"I see," Bolan said, dismissing his thoughts of a few days off to go white-water kayaking. "What kind of resources can you give me on this, Hal?"

"Very limited ones, Matt. Mr. Jacobs is right—this has to be quick and quiet and invisible, if at all possible. The U.S. can't be seen to have any official involvement or the already tenuous relations that we have with Madagascar will disintegrate. I believe the exact words were to the effect that any military actions would be considered an act of war."

"The good news is that you won't be going alone, Mr... Striker," Jacobs cut in. "We will be sending a trained operative to assist you with your mission."

"I don't think you understand the situation, Mr. Jacobs," Bolan said. "I'm an associate of Hal's. I don't take on assistants or apprentices. I work alone."

"Nevertheless, on this mission, you'll have help—like it or not." There was a scuffle of noise and a door slamming and then Brognola picked up the phone.

"I'm sorry about that, Striker. Politics, you know."

"Yeah, I got it."

"That was good work on the situation in Mexico, by the way," he said. "That should slow them down in that area for a while anyway."

"There's always another drug lord," Bolan said. "Someone will take his place. We obviously have more pressing issues at the moment."

"Someone will, and yes, we do, but I wanted to thank you anyway. The field reports on *El Varacco* made it clear he was a very unpleasant individual."

Bolan shrugged. There were a lot of unpleasant people in the world. "He was a pig, but the real danger was his second. Not that it matters, since they're both dead."

Brognola was silent for a moment, and Bolan could picture him sitting wherever he was, that sharp look of contemplation on his face. His old friend saw the world as it was, and it wasn't like him to be this hesitant during their conversations.

"What's the problem, Hal?"

"Let's finish up on Mexico first," he said after a long pause. "Early assessments from our local asset on the police force indicate that his entire organization has started to collapse."

"Good," he said. "Maybe it will take a while for someone else to pick up the pieces."

"Is there anything else of interest you need to tell me from this last mission?" Brognola asked.

"Nothing earth-shattering," Bolan said. "It's gotten pretty bad down there, and the Mexican government is trying to crack down on it. They're spread too thin, though, between enforcing their own brand of immigration justice on the southern end of the country while trying to control the flow out of the country in the north. The whole border bears watching. It's only a matter of time until it blows. They're going to have to declare martial law to keep any kind of order at all."

"That sounds about right," the big Fed said. "We've got a lot of people down there, but this mission you just completed will help—at least in that area—for a while."

"I hope so," Bolan said.

"Look, Striker, say the word and I'll find a few more people to go in quietly to assist on this newest mess. I know you haven't had time to even rest from the last mission, and it's just as easy to be quiet with three or four as it is with two."

"I appreciate the offer, Hal, but it sounds like I'll already have babysitting to do. Do you know anything about this guy that they are sending along?"

There was another long pause.

"Hal?"

"They gave me a file to look over."

"A file?"

"Yeah, but…I don't know. It's all bullshit, Striker."

"You think they're sending some kind of pencil pusher or something? Someone to keep an eye on the politics?"

"No," Brognola replied. "I think they're sending someone who doesn't exist. Someone whose cover is as deep or deeper than yours. Watch your back on this one, Striker. I've got a bad feeling that we don't have all the information and at least some of it is being kept from us."

Bolan pulled out his matched pair of Desert Eagles and snapped a clip of .44 caliber rounds into each pistol.

"You know me, Hal, I take every precaution."

Brognola chuckled softly. "Listen, the President would like to try to keep the body count low on this. I'll make an effort to let you get some downtime after this mission, but even your vacations tend to run up the numbers in the morgue."

Bolan grinned. "If you'd send me on a mission to infiltrate the set of Sesame Street, I could keep things quieter. Otherwise, I'm forced to muddle through the best I can."

"Best of luck on this one, Striker."

Bolan hung up the phone and mulled over his options for support in-country. There was one name that kept running around in his mind, but he was unwilling to accept it initially. There were too many potential complications. But the more he thought about it, the more he realized that his choices for that particular part of the world were thin. He opened a secure connection to the Stony Man Farm database and pulled up a contact name. Dusana Imrich.

He let his mind wander to the last time he'd seen her. She'd once been an agent for the CIA, working in the Balkans and the hellholes that made up Croatia and the former Czech Republic. She turned out to be not a double agent, but a triple agent, her betrayals all motivated by the fact that her family was being held prisoner by one of the warlords running the country.

She'd backstabbed Bolan, and he'd chased her all the way to Madagascar. The two of them had played a game of cat and mouse that nearly cost him his life. In the end, her situation had been revealed and it was Bolan who helped her save her family and start over on the small island. For a time, they'd been casual lovers, but that didn't mean he trusted her. He'd let her live and convinced Brognola not to let the Company know where she was.

And there was her name again. Dusana Imrich. In truth, he'd forced himself to stop thinking about her when they agreed to break it off. Anything more than a casual affair led to weaknesses he couldn't afford. He wouldn't allow a woman to be used against him ever again. He was content with his relationship with Barbara Price. He enjoyed her company when he could, but that didn't stop him from being intimate with other women. A warrior didn't know if he'd live from one day to the next and took his comfort where he could. Nothing was permanent but death.

He picked up the phone and dialed, waiting two rings before her seductively attractive voice came over the space between them. "Yes?"

"Hello, Dusana," he said. "It's good to hear your voice."

"Striker!" she exclaimed. "I don't believe it. It has been a long time."

"It has," he agreed. "How've you been?"

She laughed. "You didn't call me to ask how I've been. Not after this long."

"You caught me," he admitted. "I have a mission to take on in your part of the world and I could use some local support. Are you up for it?"

A pregnant paused filled the air as he waited for her reply. He could hear gunfire in the background and wondered if it was a problem in the making or normal for her situation these days.

"Maybe we can help each other," she said.

"Got yourself in a bind?" he asked.

"Nothing I can't handle, but another gun—especially one as big as yours—might be helpful. Hold on a moment." There was more rapid fire in the background and he could hear that she was running to change position.

The phone clunked against what sounded like concrete. He could hear yelling, but not quite make out what they were saying. Three rounds were fired closer to the phone, and Bolan had to assume they came from her weapon. Her breathy voice came back over the phone.

"So, when should I expect you?"

5

The Executioner pulled the black Hummer into the private parking area next to the tarmac, and watched the strange ballet of the airplane being fueled, pilots doing checks and ground crew moving around to ensure that all was well. Standing near a black limousine next to the plane were two men in black suits. Bolan stepped out of the Hummer, grabbed his gear and handed the keys to a waiting attendant, never taking his eyes from two men waiting for him.

In Bolan's experience, there were a lot of things that could make a mission go bad, but among the worst were bad intelligence, good people who thought they knew what they were doing—and didn't—and bad people who knew what they were doing and didn't care who got hurt. Government and corporate suits often fell into the last two categories and were regularly responsible for the first.

The two men stopped their whispered conversation as he approached. Bolan recognized Cecil Emritis, the Secretary of the Interior, and nodded politely when he stood before him. "Mr. Secretary."

"You must be Mr. Cooper," he said, not bothering to offer his hand. "Hal Brognola brought me up to speed."

Bolan contemplated the man's presence carefully. "Then you must be speeding right along, sir, because I wasn't briefed that I would be meeting you here. How can I help you?"

"Please, take no offense, Mr. Cooper. Hal wasn't made aware that I would be attending, but Arlen Foster is a close, personal friend of mine, as well as a vital member of the administration. I would consider myself remiss if I didn't take a direct hand in the efforts to extract him from the situation he's in." He turned and gestured briefly at the other man. "This is Mr. Smith."

Mr. Smith stepped forward out of the shadows, and Bolan knew instantly that this was a dangerous man. In some ways, he was even more dangerous than the Executioner himself, because Smith would be the kind of man to take on any job, no matter how dirty, without ever questioning the orders or the morality of the situation. He was a ghost, of course. Officially, he didn't exist, which meant that he could disappear and no one would look for him. He'd probably changed his name and his face so many times that whoever he'd once been was long forgotten. The two men eyed each other warily.

"Mr. Cooper," Smith said. "I can see that you're as excited as I am about having a new partner."

"I can see we're beginning to understand each other already then," Bolan replied. "I'm sure that you aren't offended, it's just that I usually work alone. Different operating styles and all that. You understand, of course."

Smith shrugged. "Of course. Sadly, I don't believe you'll have any better luck than I did convincing the powers that be that these kinds of missions are best left to a solo operative. I imagine your boss has the same deaf ears on the matter that mine does."

"I wouldn't say deaf ears, but certainly stubborn. Why don't we just try and stay out of each other's way?"

Secretary Emritis cleared his throat gruffly. "Now see here, Mr. Cooper. I understand that your boss may be Hal and that you're a special operative, but this operation is under my direction. You will follow Mr. Smith's directives."

Bolan offered him a cocked eyebrow and shook his head. "No," he replied, keeping his voice even.

The secretary's face wrinkled as angry red spread across his pompous visage. "What do you mean 'no'?"

"It's the opposite of yes," Bolan said. "I've been given my orders, Mr. Secretary, and if they change, it comes from either Hal or the President, but those are the only two men I take orders from. If you'd like to get either of them on the phone for a conversation about it, I'm happy to listen, but if not, I have a plane to catch."

Bolan waited a moment while the man sputtered in outrage, but he didn't reach for his phone, either. "That's about what I thought," he said. "Good evening, Mr. Secretary." He turned and walked past the fuming man, climbing on board the aircraft. Glancing back, he saw the secretary whispering urgently to Mr. Smith and waving his arms around. Every mission had its own dangers, but Bolan wondered if, on this one, the dangers would begin before he even got to a safe cruising altitude.

A couple of minutes passed, and then Smith strolled onto the plane. Bolan placed a Desert Eagle on the seat next to his thigh. As Smith walked by, he noted the motion and grinned. "I don't think you'll be needing that for a while yet," he said.

"I spent a lot of time in the Boy Scouts," Bolan replied. "I believe in being prepared."

"Suit yourself," Smith replied, tossing his kit onto one seat and settling into another directly across from the soldier.

"Your boss seemed a bit upset out there," Bolan said.

"You pushed his buttons," Smith replied. "Not a lot of people are willing to do that to the Secretary of the Interior."

"He's a politician. They're easily riled."

Smith looked at him carefully for a moment, then said, "Some politicians are lambs, Mr. Cooper, but some are lions."

"You forgot snakes," Bolan said.

Smith laughed quietly and nodded. "I'm simply suggesting that you should be careful of who you rile, Mr. Cooper. Lion or snake, a bite can still be fatal."

THE PRIVATE JET that took them on the long flight to Madagascar was certainly comfortable enough, but the flight took critical time off the clock, and the size of the aircraft demanded two stops for refueling. Rather than focus on his growing impatience, Bolan used the time to consider his new companion, Mr. Smith.

Though very little conversation passed between them, he was certain that Smith was as much his name as Bolan's name was Cooper. That didn't bother him half as much as his gut instinct that Smith was an executioner of an entirely different kind, but who had he been assigned to eliminate? Either way, he wasn't the kind of man you normally sent on a rescue mission into hostile territory. Smith wasn't a soldier in the traditional sense, though Bolan sensed he would be perfectly capable of handling himself.

He's the kind of man you send, he thought, for a hands-on killing—when the job called for the personal touch that left no doubt about your intentions.

Shaking his head, Bolan scanned his phone for intelligence from Brognola and reviewed the core data that he'd been given. There was little about the island nation of Madagascar that was straightforward. An ethnically and religiously diverse population, with a mountainous jungle terrain inland and a coastline that ranged from tourist- to pirate-friendly, it was a nation of contradictions. The current government wasn't popular with many of its own people, and several armed militias had gained a foothold and conducted guerrilla-style raids, particularly in the capital city. Reports conflicted as to who was on what side, and solid intelligence was almost nonexistent. It would be, in other words, a horribly mired swamp to try to get to the Secretary of State and then get him out unharmed.

He'd asked Brognola to dig up any current information on Dusana Imrich, but the reports were spotty. She was known as a player, and one report potentially linked her to the assassination of a high-ranking government official, but it appeared that, for the most part, she'd been flying under the radar. Before he left, he'd sent her a list of equipment to try to put together, but there was no telling if any of it was available.

Bolan looked again at his traveling companion. They would be landing soon and he knew that he would have to at least pretend to play nice until he knew what Smith's real agenda was. There was little that he trusted, but the more he could get Smith to talk, the better. He moved across the aircraft and sat across from Smith with his newest phone device in hand. Among other things, the small computer could broadcast a small, holographic image in 3D. Bolan pulled up a schematic of the island. A bright yellow dot showed the last known coordinates of the Secretary of State at the airport.

"Pretty fancy toy you have there," Smith observed.

"I've learned to adapt to technology, especially when it can give me an edge. This modeling software works well to plan an extraction."

"Hmm…yes. I assume you have some thoughts on that."

Deciding to try a direct approach, Bolan nodded. "We've got limited information, but before we start talking plans, I'd like to know what I'm missing."

"Missing?" Smith asked.

"Yeah," he replied. "What's your role in this?"

"Pretty much the same as yours, unless you're getting at something else. Are you?"

"Look," Bolan said, "I don't buy that you're here because the SoS is a personal friend of Emritis. The mission was approved as a solo extraction by the President. It doesn't require two, so why are you really here?"

Smith shrugged, all innocence and nonchalance. "You'd have to ask my boss of the day. I go where I'm told and do the job they tell me to do. That's it."

Bolan watched him carefully. There were no obvious signs of deception, but for a pro like Smith, there wouldn't be. He would need careful watching until his real agenda was revealed. He punched a code into his phone, and the image switched to a topographical overlay. Three small red spots were added to the image.

"So, what are the dots?"

"The yellow one is the airport, where the secretary was taken. Those other three are the known locations of militia camps. The problem is that there are multiple militias in the area—we think these are the ones who took the secretary—but worse, the main base is unknown, and these camps are mobile. That means by the time we get to them, they could be gone. Still, they're probably the best place to start."

Smith pointed to the red dot farthest from the city. "That one there is in the middle of the jungle. Do you have a way in?"

"I have some resources, but nothing concrete yet. What about you?"

"I make my own resources."

The captain turned on the public address system and announced, "Gentlemen, we'll be on the ground in just a few minutes. Everything looks clear. If you aren't seated and belted in, now's the time."

Bolan disabled the phone and stored it in the pocket of the tactical vest he was wearing. He returned to his seat, buckled up and leaned over to look at the airport through the window. The clouds made the island gray and foreboding as they landed, and the trees on the far edge of the field sagged under the weight of the water in the air. He turned his attention back to Smith just as the plane touched down on the rough tarmac.

"We'll be taxiing for a couple of minutes," the captain said. "Then we'll be stopping at the hangar."

Bolan and Smith unbuckled their seat belts and stood at the same time, each reaching for his gear bag.

The first clue that anything was wrong was the shattering explosion of the rocket smashing into the cockpit of the plane. The impact was enough to knock both men nearly off their feet, and the blast of superheated air that washed through the cabin was enough to tell them that the pilot was dead.

Slinging his duffel bag over his shoulder, Bolan said, "Emergency exit in the back," then moved for it without waiting for Smith.

A second blast took out the wing on the far side of the plane, and Bolan silently offered thanks that there wasn't a lot of fuel left in the craft to add to the mayhem. As it was, the air was hot enough to burn going into his lungs. He hit the emergency exit door at almost full speed, yanking open the handle and shoving the door aside as the slide inflated and deployed.

Almost immediately, the soldiers opened fire, and bullets smashed into the side of the plane with the thudding pings of assault rifle slugs. "No good," he said, diving behind the heavy door for cover.

Smith had taken a position in the galley, using the metal service cart for cover. "You have any other ideas?" he called. "It's getting pretty damn hot in here."

Bolan's mind raced as he considered the possibilities and the layout of the plane. "Only one, but you're not going to like it."

"I like getting shot or burned alive even less," Smith replied.

Bolan dropped to the floor and began to crawl back to

the front of the plane. He heard Smith curse behind him, but he felt his reluctant presence behind him as they made their way to the avionics hatch at the front of the plane. Bullets tore through the bulkhead as they moved, covering them with debris and shards of broken glass from the windows. The intense heat of the fire roared around them as Bolan shrugged off the burning pieces of the bulkhead, which was slowly collapsing around them. He reached for the hatch, but the searing heat of the metal had him yanking his hand back. Bolan pulled out the combat knife that he kept in his boot and raked through a section of carpet, ripping it free and using it to protect his hand.

The hole in the floor was a tight fit, but as a section of the roof began to collapse there was little choice. Dropping his bag in front of him into the small cargo area, he wasted no time getting to the landing gear and peeking below. The small army surrounding them was focused on the chaos above. The Executioner took advantage of their distraction and slipped out next to the wheel with Smith hot on his heels. "Now what?" Smith asked, peering out from behind their meager cover.

"Now we fight our way out," Bolan said, grinning at him. "Unless you've got a better idea."

"None whatsoever," Smith replied, pulling his handgun free. "But we're a little outgunned and outmanned, wouldn't you say?"

Bolan shrugged as he took his Desert Eagle out of the holster on his hip. "That's nothing new," he stated, peering through the smoke.

6

If they could get to the side of the warehouse they'd have a lot more cover. There were stacks of shipping crates on pallets, barrels, and even trash cans that would give them time to fight off their attackers. Whoever they are, he added to himself. "I'll go right," he told Smith. "You go left. We'll each take one side of the warehouse and see if we can split them up a bit."

"When?" Smith asked, dodging slightly as a piece of flaming, melted plastic fell out of the hole and almost landed on his back.

"Now," Bolan said, moving in a half-crouch from beneath the plane. The Desert Eagle boomed like a cannon, and the first round he fired took out the man positioned at a turreted machine gun in the back of the closest jeep. He offered a garbled scream as he flipped over backward. He heard the higher tones of Smith's 9 mm pistol and continued firing on his own.

From the looks of it, splitting up had been the right choice. The soldiers were confused as to which man to shoot at, and their fields of fire were almost crossing into each other. Bolan rolled as a burst of rifle fire tore into the concrete at his heels, and managed to slide behind a heavy garbage bin. It was still a good thirty yards or more to the better cover at the side of the warehouse.

He saw Smith running for the far side of the building as

two men turned their attention in his direction with their AK-47s and opened fire. Bolan locked them in his sights and two shots later that particular threat to Smith was over, but unfortunately it brought more attention his way. The garbage bin was decent cover, but an even better target, and as more bullets seemed to be armor-piercing than not, the once-large shield was becoming a giant piece of Swiss cheese.

Bolan looked around for other ideas and spotted a small can of gasoline. Using the end of a broken pallet, he pulled the can closer. A bullet ricocheted off the concrete and through the piece of wood, but thankfully left the gas can intact.

Undeterred, he reached again and pulled it closer. There was enough fuel to help his cause, so Bolan pulled an old tire out from under the bin. He poured fuel over the tire and then sat the can in the middle before setting it ablaze. The fuel wasn't enough to cause an explosion, but the burning tire created an effective smoke shield in the slight wind, giving him the advantage. Bolan fired several rounds through the smoke, hitting one man by the sounds of it and giving the soldiers ample opportunity to reconsider chasing him through the haze.

Making a mad dash for the side of the warehouse, Bolan heard the sound of yet another jeep approaching his position. This was not the quiet, stealthy entrance into Madagascar he'd hoped for, and the situation was rapidly spiraling out of control. He'd already lost sight of Smith in the chaos and wondered where the man had gone. Finding cover behind a double-stacked row of shipping crates, he paused for breath and to assess the scene again, when he realized that the soldiers who'd attacked the plane weren't paying any attention to him at all.

The newest arrival wasn't an enemy, but Dusana Imrich and another man, driving hell-for-leather across the tarmac, as she opened up with an M60 on full-auto. Soldiers ran into each other, screaming and dropping their weapons—some dying—as she strafed the area with heavy rounds. The woman was as dangerous as he remembered, but for the moment, she was a white knight on a fiery steed and despite the role reversal, Bolan planned to take full advantage of the situation. He reloaded the Desert Eagle and charged forward.

The first man he met died before he even knew Bolan was there, and the second almost got his gun up as the Executioner's round took him low in the throat. Imrich's M60 finally wound down just as Bolan got back to the front end of what was left of their plane. He grabbed his duffel bag and tossed it into the jeep, while she used an assault rifle to keep the enemy pinned down.

A quick glance told him that their attackers had decided to cut and run, the few who were left anyway, heading back into the warehouse. The man he'd seen barking orders earlier lay facedown in a widening pool of blood.

"Need a ride, soldier?" Imrich asked.

"Anywhere but here," he said. "But I'm missing someone."

"Who?" she asked.

"I had an extra with me—calls himself Smith—but he disappeared early in the fight."

"I have the manpower to get you the hell out, not to go farther in."

"You know I can't do that, Dusana."

"I know, I know. It's always a suicide mission with you. Climb aboard and we'll try to track down your friend." She spoke rapid-fire French to the driver, who gunned the engine as Bolan jumped into the jeep.

They headed around the edge of the warehouse. The side was clear initially, but two pickups with mounted M60s were headed their direction. Bolan took aim, taking out the first gunner, and Imrich injured the second. They ran past each other, but the two trucks weren't about to give up pursuit and three jeeps were now coming their way.

The bullets started to fly and their driver was hit, sending the jeep out of control into the oncoming assault. Bolan dropped down and reached for the wheel, trying to steady the vehicle. The driver was hit again, his head whipping back with the impact of the bullet. Out of options, Bolan shoved the dead body out of the jeep and slid in behind the wheel, firing the Desert Eagle with one hand as he changed gears with the other. Gunning the engine, he drove straight at the enemy.

"What the hell are you doing?" Imrich yelled.

"Killing bad guys," he said, taking aim through the shattered window and firing another round into an exposed militiaman's chest. "Why aren't you?"

As Bolan suspected, the three approaching vehicles began to slow and the other two trucks were picking up speed behind him. Bolan sped up and, at the last second, slammed on the brakes, spinning the jeep in a circle, nearly flipping as he did so. He fired two shots into the tires of one of the oncoming vehicles.

It rocked out of control, rolled, and took out one of the trucks that had been hot on their heels. Imrich fired off three more shots and pulled out two grenades. Bolan let his pursuers get a little closer and then locked up the brakes, bringing one of the jeeps alongside them. Imrich pulled the pins and lobbed the grenades into the open top of the jeep. Bolan floored the gas pedal and pulled away as the dual explosions rocked behind them.

The move didn't seem to deter the others so much as spur them on. Bolan spun and caught a glimpse of Smith shimmying over the fence on the far side of the airstrip and knew he was safe, at least for the moment. The man really was a ghost, but so far, not all that helpful when the bullets started flying.

"Was that him?" Imrich asked.

"Yeah, I think so."

"Then what do you say we get the hell out of here?" she suggested. "I'd rather catch up over a glass of wine than while people are shooting at us."

"Sounds like a good plan to me," he said.

She pulled out two smoke grenades, armed them and threw the smokers in their wake. As they went off, she pulled an M16 from the floor and fired through the smoke.

"I wonder where you learned that trick," Bolan said, smiling.

"Just something I once picked up from a man with a big gun," she retorted, grinning back at him.

THE STEAMY HEAT of Antananarivo, the capital city of Madagascar, was oppressive—especially on days like this one, when there was no breeze at all from the ocean. They left the jeep at an empty warehouse several miles from the airport and walked deeper into the city. Several blocks in, a dilapidated taxi pulled up, and Imrich said, "Our ride is here." She moved to the driver's window and spoke quickly to him, then waved for Bolan to come over. At his reticence, she laughed and grabbed his hand, all but dragging him toward the cab.

The small yellow cab had seen many better days. The paint was faded, chipped and generally worn. The windows were dirty and in two places had obviously been struck by small-caliber bullets. One of the taillights was broken out, and red tape was plastered in place over the bulb instead of the sturdy clouded plastic that adorned the opposite side. A rosary and a small statue of the Virgin Mary hung from the rearview mirror. The tires, he noted, were completely bald. By any measure, the thing looked like death on wheels.

Bolan opened the trunk and tossed his duffel bag in, then shut it firmly. He opened the back door and guided Imrich inside, climbing in behind her and then shutting the door. It latched, if only out of habit. The driver was gazing at them in the rearview mirror and offered a slight grin from his dark-skinned face.

"All right, Gabriel," Imrich said. "You've had a good look, now get going."

Gabriel laughed and put the car in gear with an alarming rattle of metal from the transmission. It lurched into motion.

"I take it you know each other?" Bolan asked

Imrich nodded. "Gabriel here knows more secrets about 'Rivo than anyone I've ever met. I pay him enough to share *most* of them with me."

Bolan looked once more at the disreputable taxi. "Maybe you should pay him enough to get a new cab."

"This one suits him and makes him all but invisible in the worst neighborhoods."

"Good point," he admitted.

He watched Imrich as she settled into the seat next to him. It had been a long time since he'd seen her, but she was just as beautiful as he remembered. Long dark hair that hung in light curls almost to her waist, high breasts and slight hips. She was wearing a black tank top that showed almost as much as it covered, and he could see that she was still in excellent shape. Her arms were muscled, and down her right biceps a stylized jungle cat wrapped around her arm. She smiled and ran her finger along his thigh. Bolan looked down at her hand and raised an eyebrow.

"I've missed you, Cooper. We were always good together. I've got dinner reservations for us later, but I thought you would want to clean up first."

"This isn't a social visit, Dusana. We have work to do."

She leaned into him and placed a light kiss below his ear, rubbing her hand on his chest.

"You never are, but you have to eat, showers are never

a bad thing on assignment and I never could resist you, especially after a little action."

Seeing her again brought back a lot of memories. And the simple truth was that he wanted her.

As the cab pulled up to the hotel, Bolan handed Gabriel some bills and jumped out. Gabriel popped the trunk from up front and Bolan grabbed his duffel bag and headed into the hotel with Imrich.

The sexual tension between them grew to an almost unbearable heat as they entered the elevator and rode up to the eleventh floor. Imrich slid the key card through the door slot and opened it. A moment later, with no additional words, they were pulling each other's clothing off.

Bolan smiled as he slid his hand past the waistband of her cargo pants and found no other garment impeding his progress. She smiled and slid back onto the bed, pulling Bolan down with her. There were moments where names and titles no longer mattered; he wasn't an agent or a soldier, just a man with a beautiful woman.

For the moment, that was enough.

7

"I've missed you, Matt," Imrich said. "And I'm sorry for not getting in touch with you sooner." She was curled up against him, still sweating from their exertions, and couldn't have looked more inviting if she'd tried.

"You've gone some ways toward making it up to me," he said. "And I missed you, too, Dusana. But considering that we hadn't really talked in two years until I called you, I can be excused for thinking that I wasn't still on your mind. We made our decision at the time in good faith."

"You can, of course. I understand. But it wasn't that I wasn't thinking about you or didn't want to see you. It's just that…since I came down here, life got more than a little complicated and we both knew the risks of being together. I knew you never really could make a long-term plan."

"Nothing about that has changed, Dusana. I am who I am, and so far, I still have a job to do. The missions may change, but the job—and my duty—stay the same. While I still can do it, and while there's still a need, I'll do what I have to do."

"Same old Matt," she said, chuckling. "Still talking about duty. But I didn't expect anything else, and that's fair enough."

"You didn't come to the airport and pull me out of a firefight for sex, and when we spoke on the phone it sounded like things were very complicated. What's going on with you?"

"Ah, I've missed your directness," she said, laughing. "You don't let me get away with anything do you?"

"Sometimes," he said.

"Isn't it obvious?" she asked. "You haven't put it all together yet?"

"Like I said, the sex is nice, but either one of us can get laid anytime we want without the travel and the gunplay. I'm glad for your help on this mission, but my gut tells me that your interest is more than lending me a hand or helping with my 'gun.'"

"You know that what we had was never just about sex or guns of either type," she said. "But you're right. This is about so much more than that. In the end, maybe it's about freedom."

Bolan climbed out of bed and walked over to the bar. "Something to drink?" he asked.

"Sure," she said. "There's cold beer in the minifridge."

"Sounds good," he replied. He found the beer, a local brand he didn't recognize, and opened two bottles, pouring them into glasses from behind the bar. She wrapped a sheet tightly around herself as he came back to the bed, silently handing her the beer. He sat on the edge of the bed and took a long swallow of his own. The beer was ice cold, slightly fruity and delicious on his tongue. Bolan had a feeling he would need the fortification to hear whatever it was she had to say. Dusana Imrich was a beautiful woman, but her thought process could be as deadly as her aim. When it came to politics her views were all mixed with what happened to her family, and it never made for a clear picture.

Imrich settled herself, setting the glass on the nightstand. "What do you know about what's really happening here in Madagascar?"

"Not as much as I'd like for a mission like this. The field intelligence we have is pretty sketchy in this part of the world.

The government is at odds with its people, and the militia groups seem to be everywhere and nowhere. Uprisings in the jungle, that sort of thing."

She nodded. "That's about the scope of it—as far as the intelligence reports go. There are more details than you have in your databases, but at least you have a frame of reference."

"Go on," Bolan said.

"You and I both know that there are at least three sides to every story, Matt, and when it comes down to working in the field, we never have a full picture until we're already there, right?"

"True enough," he said. "The situation on the ground is always different, to some degree, compared to the advance intelligence. What are you driving at, Dusana?"

"Nothing is simple in Madagascar, certainly not here in 'Rivo," she said. "You know that as well as I do. But maybe the best way to make my point is in comparison."

"Go on."

"There are two men. One is an evil man who plots and schemes, takes money from the poor and lines his own pockets with it. He bends others to his will, and when they don't bend, he has no compunction about breaking them, torturing them, or killing them—or their families."

"I assume you mean Velona."

Marc Velona was known as a ruthless leader who went unchallenged by anyone in his government. Anyone who tried either disappeared or had a sudden change of heart. The regime was powerful, but like all regimes there were flaws, and the rebels often exploited those.

"Yes, Velona. He's created a government so corrupt that the idea of one person bearing it, let alone an entire country, is insupportable."

"I don't disagree, but why are we discussing things that

we both already know. I have a mission here, Dusana, and the clock is ticking. Tell me you've got a point to make here."

"Never fear, darling. There is a point. The other man. The man who would rid this country of Velona and make it free again."

"And that would be?"

"He's…not what the intelligence reports would have you believe, though I leaked a number of the details in them myself."

"So…does this mystery man have a name or do I have to guess? Are you working for him?"

"Yes and no."

Imrich paused for a long moment and stared at him. Bolan had sudden sense of foreboding. His instincts started moving into overdrive and he began to notice everything, how far they each were to a door, the sounds of the people in the hallway. He tried to shake the feeling, but it wouldn't go away.

She shook her head. "I don't think that telling you will work, I have to show you what I'm getting at."

"What have you gotten yourself into, Dusana?"

"A new beginning for Madagascar. This is my home now, my new family. As I said, I need to show you."

"You're making me nervous, and I'm trying to connect the dots here. I need to find the Secretary of State, and you're talking about some local militiaman who's going to take out Velona. Are they connected?"

"In some ways, yes."

"You know I don't like mysteries, Dusana, and what if I don't like what it is that you have to show me?" He gave her a hard stare.

"Nothing happens," she said, trying to reassure him. "You are free to continue on your mission and I'll still help you, but I believe many of the answers that you're looking for will reveal themselves if you're just willing to trust me."

Bolan didn't laugh out loud, but the thought of trusting anyone who spoke in riddles was ridiculous. Unfortunately, she was the only resource he had at the moment. Sometimes you just had to go in blind and make do any way you could. She wasn't the type to waste his time—at least, he didn't think so.

"All right, Dusana. Show me whatever it is you've got to show me, but if you're wasting my time…"

"I'm not, Matt. This is important. Just trust me a little further."

She got up off of the bed, went to her garment bag and pulled out a wide black tie. She turned, holding it in her hand.

"We're going to dinner?"

"No, I'm going to blindfold you."

Bolan inwardly cringed. Going in blind metaphorically was one thing, but doing it literally was another matter.

"What? You don't think you can trust me?" she asked. She strolled forward and began to slip it around his eyes.

"I understand the precaution, but why now?"

Bolan tensed as she put her hand on his chest. She pushed him back onto the bed and climbed onto his lap letting the sheet slide to the floor.

"We're going to practice our game of trust in advance. Sometimes, Cooper, you just need to go along for the ride."

BOLAN DIDN'T ENJOY the sensation of flying along through the jungle in a jeep blindfolded, but he forced himself to relax. Whatever his companion was up to, he knew she wouldn't harm him—and that she wanted his support. They took several twists and turns, and ten minutes into the ride, he was completely disoriented. Imrich continued driving the jeep for more than an hour longer before she brought it to a stop.

"Okay," she said. "You can take off the blindfold."

Bolan pulled it away from his eyes and blinked several

times in the filtered golden sunlight that poured through the breaks in the towering trees. In front of them, a large cream-colored adobe wall marked the edges of some kind of military compound. Even parked outside the heavy, reinforced gates, he could see guards patrolling the top of the wall, and two men stationed in a watch tower. Along the top of the wall, floodlights were regularly spaced, as were electronic eyes that—when activated—would use lasers to detect intruders.

"*This* is what you wanted to show me?" he asked. "It's a good-looking wall, but you and I both know that walls are only as good as the men who guard them."

Imrich chuckled. "Same old Cooper. You never pull your punches, do you?"

"Not as often as most people would like," he said. "You included."

She shrugged. "Fair enough. But what I think will really interest you is on the inside." She honked the horn and the gates swung open.

"A horn-based security system?" he asked. Imrich put the jeep in gear and drove through into the courtyard beyond. As she cleared the gates, she hit the horn again and the gates swung shut behind them. "Not the horn," she said. "Frequency modulated sound waves controlled by a remote computer. If one of our jeeps goes missing, we simply change the frequency on all of them except the missing one. Presto— the locks are redone."

"A nice touch," he admitted. "That's some pretty heavy-duty tech for…what? A little militia in the middle of nowhere?"

"You'll see," she said, parking the jeep at the end of a row of identical vehicles. All of them looked to be well-maintained and up to military spec. She climbed out of the driver's seat. "Come on, Cooper," she said. "I'll show you everything. I think you'll be impressed, and you'll understand why I've asked you here."

He stepped out of the jeep and grabbed his duffel bag from the back, his eyes sweeping the courtyard. The men on the walls patrolled in two-man teams, and though he couldn't see the back wall, a quick count revealed at least fourteen soldiers along the front and one side. The courtyard itself was laid out in military fashion and with an eye toward defense. There was plenty of cover, provided by small fountains cleverly disguised to look ornamental but that were very functional places to lay down covering fire.

A long, low building made out of the same fire-resistant adobe appeared to be barracks, and another one looked like some kind of storage building. Both of them were designed for functionality, rather than style, but the main house was a different story. It was on two levels and similar in style to some of the more contemporary Southwestern designs. A large set of stairs led up to double doors. Windows looked out on the courtyard and the jungle, but were covered by heavy bars that looked stylish. Bolan knew at a glance that they were strong enough to make breaking in—or out—very difficult. Hidden within little outcroppings of adobe or behind plants, he saw the telltale glimmer of cameras.

"Get a good look?" Imrich asked.

"Sure," he said. "You designed all this, didn't you?"

"Down to the flagstones you're standing on," she said. "It's been a long project."

"Weapons hidden in the fountains?" he asked.

She laughed softly, and for a moment, Bolan could see in his mind's eye their first days together. He shook his head slightly, banishing the memory. He wasn't sure what the woman was up to, but with all that he'd seen so far, it couldn't be good.

"What have you got going on here, Dusana?"

"A lot," she admitted. "Let me show you the main house."

She headed for the wide stairway that led to the front doors, her long legs eating up ground rapidly.

Bolan kept pace, noting as they ascended that the height of each stair was slightly shorter than normal. If a person was used to it, it wouldn't be noticed, but trying to run up or down them in the dark would cause a lot of people to trip and fall. Imrich had always had an eye for detail and this was one of a probably a hundred or more little ways she'd turned this complex into a potential deathtrap for enemies. They reached the doors and she stopped.

"Just a moment," she said. Sliding aside a metal plate, she put her palm on a scanner. It flared briefly as it read her handprint.

"Access granted," a quiet voice said. The doors unlocked with a fairly loud clunking noise.

Internal bars, Bolan thought. "What, no retinal scanner?" he quipped.

"Not quite yet," she said. "For now, we have to make do with the hand scanners, but someday soon, perhaps." She pulled open one of the doors—they opened outward, yet another defensive detail—and led him through the doorway. The entryway was octagon-shaped, with patterned tile on the floors and native tapestries on the walls. On either side of the doorway, at three different heights, he spotted the projectors for tiny lasers that would be attached to the alarm system, but he didn't see the control mechanism.

Noting his gaze, she said, "The control panel isn't here, Cooper. It's in the security room."

He nodded. "Makes sense."

"Come on," she said, taking his arm lightly. "Oh, and leave your bag here. I'll have Maria take care of it."

"Are we staying?" he asked.

"I hope so," she said. "But that will depend on what you think when I've shown you everything."

"You never fail to surprise," he said. But inwardly, Bolan knew that whatever she was into probably wouldn't be good for him—or his mission.

8

Bolan dropped his duffel bag with a muffled thump. "Lead on," he said. "You've got my attention."

"Good," she replied, moving into the open area beyond the entryway. To their right was a large living room, with heavy Spanish furniture, a stone fireplace and a wet bar with crystal decanters along the top. One wall contained a huge bookshelf that was filled from top to bottom.

To their left was a dining room, and Imrich headed in that direction. Wall hangings and native masks decorated the walls. The table was a dark wood, polished to a high gloss. Fresh-cut flowers in a crystal vase were placed on a delicate doily in the table's middle. The chairs were high-backed and armless, and looked like antiques, based on the scrollwork. She barely slowed as they moved through the room to the doorway on the far side.

Imrich paused there, and peered through the saloon-style doors into the kitchen beyond. A local woman stood over a stove stirring something in a large stockpot. She caught a glimpse of Imrich out of the corner of her eye.

"Dusana!" she said, turning in their direction and setting down the metal ladle. "You've brought him!" Her smile was bright and lit up her entire face. Bolan guessed her age to be mid to late fifties, but her manner was that of someone much younger.

Even as she said, "Nice to meet you," Bolan found himself wrapped in a warm hug.

"Dusana has told me so much about you," she said, releasing the hug and holding him at arm's length. "I'm glad you are here."

"Come on, Cooper. Let me show you the rest of the house and introduce you. If you're going to survive one of Maria's feasts, you'll need to work up an appetite." She kissed Maria on the cheek and said, "Can you have Cooper's bag taken to my room, please? It's in the entryway."

"Sassy girl," Maria said. "Yes, it will be done." Then, without another word, the woman skittered back into the kitchen.

"She's charming," Bolan said.

"You'll never meet a nicer woman and she's been an important part of my life. It's great that I was able to find a place for her here—it's safer than working in the city and good work."

"Safer?" he asked.

"Velona," she muttered darkly, and then shrugged. "But enough of that for now. Plenty of time to talk about the problems we're dealing with. For right now, let's get you oriented."

"Fine," he said, wanting to believe that all would be well, but fearing that whatever it was Dusana had gotten herself into would be nothing but bad news for him.

Bolan was surprised at the tenderness that she showed Maria. After all of the heartache that Dusana went through with her own family, she'd been pretty hard-hearted when it came to people she didn't know or trust. But this place... seeing her interact with Maria was a side of her he'd thought long dead.

The reports of how the government was treating the people were a shadow of the reality that Dusana was presenting.

Bolan was a pragmatist and knew how most governments operated. Some killed openly and some killed in secret, and many of them killed or controlled or enslaved their own people. They did it with guns and money and laws.

Frankly, Bolan had come to realize that he couldn't go to war with every government or person who treated people badly. He had to choose his battles, keeping an eye on the bigger picture and trying to make a difference in the long run. Still, it was good to see her actually care about someone in the sense of a true family.

Imrich led him back to the main entry and pointed down the hallway on either side of the stairs that led to the second floor. "The left hallway leads to a restroom—first door on your left—and Maria's room is at the end of the hall. On the right is my office and bedroom.

"Right now, let's go upstairs." She bounded up the steps, half dragging him along. The landing at the top of the stairs split to the left and the right. Imrich turned left. The hallway stopped almost immediately at a large door. Imrich paused and rapped twice on the door.

"Enter," a deep, masculine voice called from the other side.

She opened the door and they stepped inside a large office. On the balcony was a man with his back to them. He was broad-shouldered and lean at the waist, but even with his stiff, military posture, Bolan could see that he was muscular. His uniform was similar to that worn by the outside guards: black pants tucked into boots and a pressed khaki shirt. He turned to face them, and Bolan noted that his insignia was nothing more than a simple row of small, silver stars along his collar with another set of them on his black beret. His boots were U.S. military jungle boots, buffed to a high gloss.

"Ah, Dusana," he said. "I thought I heard you arrive." He moved into the room, comfortably turning his back to the jungle beyond his compound. He had the dark complexion, hair and eyes so common to people from this part of the world, and wore a neatly trimmed mustache. "This must be Cooper, whom you've spoken so highly of." He stepped closer and offered his hand.

Bolan returned the handshake and noticed that the man's grip was firm and his hands callused. This wasn't a paper general, but a working soldier, despite the clean lines of his uniform. "Matt Cooper," he said.

"General Arland Rija," he replied, "at your service."

The name hit him like a thunderbolt, though he did his best to hide the reaction. The name Rija wasn't new to him—he'd read it in the most recent intelligence reports provided by Brognola. According to their information, he had started out as a small-time drug lord, moved into piracy in the Bay of Bengal, then slowly but surely built himself a small militia. In the past couple of years, however, he'd gone pro and was connected to, if not responsible for, a string of high-level diplomatic kidnappings. None of the victims had been harmed, but all of them had been ransomed for money or military equipment. It was rumored that Velona himself had placed a bounty on Rija's head that would be enough to retire any one of Madagascar's citizens for life and then some.

"General Rija," he said, releasing his hand. "I…find I'm surprised to meet you in person. Before this, I only knew you as a name in an intelligence report."

Both Imrich and Rija laughed.

"See what I told you?" Imrich said. "He thinks on his feet. Already he knows that you and I are connected."

"I've connected some of the dots," the big American said. "But I'm sure the picture isn't complete yet."

"Please," Rija said. "Let's sit down and have a drink." He gestured to a group of couches and chairs around a large metalwork coffee table with a glass top. "Dusana, will you do the honors?"

"Of course," she said, moving to the bar. "What can I pour for you, Rija?"

"Tequila," he said, finding a seat in one of the chairs. "Cooper?"

"The same," Bolan said, noting how Rija had chosen the power position for himself. Bolan took the chair most likely to give him room to maneuver in the event all of this turned into some kind of confrontation. Dusana had to have completely lost her mind, unless he was missing something.

"Good," Rija said. "Tequila for everyone."

Imrich poured each of them a double shot and topped Bolan's with a slice of lime. She brought over the drinks, set them on the table and took a seat on the couch. Everyone reached for a glass.

"To new friends," Rija said.

"To new friends," Bolan and Imrich replied.

All of them drank the gold-colored liquid in a smooth swallow or two, and Bolan followed his with a bite of the lime. Returning his glass to the tray on the table, he studied the two people before him. In demeanor they were similar, and it could be supposed that they were not all that different in background.

"So," Bolan said, choosing his words carefully. "Which one of you wants to explain why I'm here?"

Rija laughed again and Imrich smiled in response.

"I guess that I should start, Cooper," Imrich said. "But let me assure you that you are safe here. This isn't a trap and if you don't like what we have to say, I'll take you back to 'Rivo and no hard feelings."

"Uh-huh," he said, not really believing it.

"Of course," Rija continued, "we will require your word that nothing of what you learn here will leave with you. Dusana has told me that you would not go back on your word once given, and she has proved herself a great asset many times, so I trust *her* word that this is true."

Bolan knew that if he did anything other than agree he would likely never leave this place. "I would not betray Dusana," he said, holding his voice firm. "She's too important to me."

"Good," Rija said. "I expected nothing else. She has spoken so highly of you during these past few days that I almost feel as if I know you myself."

Reverting to form, Bolan said, "I'm a little surprised. Normally, all she talks about is herself."

Rija slapped his knee and laughed with pleasure. "He *does* know you, my dear!"

"Ha-ha," Imrich said. "He's got me pegged, all right." When the laughter died down, she said, "So, you want to know why you're here, yes?"

He nodded.

"It's pretty simple, but in order to answer that, I need to give you some background." When he didn't say anything, she continued. "What you've read in the intelligence reports about Rija is mostly true. The government got its information from me, and it made no sense to lie when the truth served our purpose much better. Yes, Rija got his start in the drug trade and he took the money from that and started building his militia. But all of it has been planned from the beginning to bring about the change needed, the critical changes that are absolutely required here in Madagascar."

"Velona," he said quietly.

"Velona," she agreed. "Velona and the men of his regime have killed hundreds, probably thousands of families here. They killed everyone in Rija's family except him, and the only reason he lived is because one of the neighbors helped hide him in the jungle."

"Why were they killed?" Bolan asked.

"They were speaking out against Velona," she said shortly. "I was on a training mission in 'Rivo and saw the damage as they dragged the bodies in from the jungle and lined them up for the photo opportunity."

"And that's how you met Rija," he guessed.

"He was already on the watch list when I got here," Imrich said. "But when I started doing the surveillance work, I realized he was doing more than selling drugs or building a private little army for his own security. He wanted to build something bigger and better. We met and I've been working for him ever since."

Bolan looked at Rija. "I wonder if you would be willing to excuse us, please?" he asked.

"You have shocked him, Dusana," Rija said, getting to his feet. He turned and offered her a little bow. "If you are as skilled as she has said, it would be an honor to have you join our cause. I will leave you alone to talk."

"Thank you," Bolan said.

"Dusana, I will be down in the security center," he said, moving toward the door. "I think you have some explaining to do."

"So it seems," Imrich replied, watching as Rija left, shutting the door behind him.

Turning to Bolan, she grinned. "Well, let's have it," she said. "You won't be happy until you do."

9

"In my line of work, there's a word for what you've done," Bolan said, giving her a hard stare.

"Traitor?" she suggested. "I know that one already."

"Rogue," he snapped. "What the hell are you thinking? I pulled you out of the fire once before Dusana. I vouched for you and it was my word via Hal Brognola that kept you alive when you betrayed the CIA. If it's found out that you've aligned yourself with this man, that you've been actively helping him of your own free will, they'll take you down like a rabid dog." He got to his feet, angrier than he'd been in a long while. "To tell you the truth, if it weren't for our past, I'd turn you in myself."

"Since when has a shared past stopped you?" she asked.

Bolan shrugged and contemplated his own words. He wasn't exaggerating. On her current path, helping a man who was not only responsible for drug and weapons smuggling and trying to overthrow a government, but kidnapping important officials for money… He shook his head, as sad as he was angry. She'd wind up on a hit list for sure. He folded his arms and leaned against the wall, trying to find his sense of balance.

Finally, he shrugged and sighed. Imrich laughed. "Cooper, you know I'm in the right here. People are suffering in this country. How can helping them—however I can—make me a rogue?"

"Because there are *rules,* Dusana," he pointed out. "We play by certain rules. We have to, because the bad guys don't. All the sentiment in the world won't be much of a comfort when people like Hal Brognola find out what you've been doing—and they will find out, you know that—and you wake up dead one morning. How will you help them then?"

"I'm not going to wake up dead, Cooper," she said, smiling gently. She got to her feet and took his hand. "That's why I asked you here. I want you to help us, help our cause."

"And how, exactly, do you want me to do that?" he asked, exasperated. It was like she couldn't see her situation objectively. "I want you to convince Washington to support us. Overthrowing Velona benefits not just this country, but the region. With the right man in power, even the Bay of Bengal will be safer."

He stared at her, incredulous, then barked a short laugh. "Convince Washington…that's more than a tall order, Dusana. It's asking the impossible. I don't exist officially, and I doubt the President will listen to Hal. We're the tools of the machine. We don't run it."

She sighed. "Cooper, I don't want all of this to be unsanctioned by the powers that be, especially in the international community. I want their blessing and so does, Rija."

"There's only one reason that Rija would want the blessing of the United States government…he wants their support if he comes to power. That's incredibly ambitious, but I have to tell you that kidnapping the Secretary of State is not the way to get the support of the government. In fact, it's a good way for all of you to get killed. Why do you think they sent me?"

"We don't have him," she said. "We never have."

"What do you mean you don't have him?" he snapped. "Rija claimed responsibility."

"We have informants in the city, and when we heard about it, we decided to use the opportunity it presented."

"So, Rija's never kidnapped anyone and used them for leverage?"

"I'm not saying that, though in this case, it wasn't us. But we knew it would be believable if Rija said it was him."

Bolan held up his hand. "Don't tell me any more, Dusana. I can't believe after everything we went through getting you out of that mess in Sarajevo…" He took a deep breath, trying to contain his disappointment. "This is simple. I have a job to do—find and rescue the Secretary of State—and that's what I'm going to do. Right now, what I need to know is if you and your 'band of brothers' here are involved."

"I told you that we aren't," she said, the color rising in her cheeks. "It was a ruse to buy notice from the U.S."

"It bought you notice, all right. It bought you me. Don't you understand? They could have just as easily sent me in to kill everyone even remotely involved, or sent in a black ops team. You'd have all been dead and no one the wiser."

Imrich looked down, nodding. "You're right, Cooper. We got lucky. I guessed when you called that they'd decided to send you, and I thought that if I helped you find the Secretary of State, it might go a long way toward our cause."

Bolan sighed again. There was no one more blind than a person fighting for a cause or a religion. "I don't work for causes, Dusana. I have missions, and I complete them. I just need to know if my current mission starts here or somewhere else."

"I already told you it doesn't start here, but I've got a pretty good idea of where it might. Kidnappings are a way of life here, and there are two places that I know of where they might have taken him. We've also got informants working the streets to see if they can hear anything, though this was so out of the blue, and so well-planned, that everyone was caught flat-footed. Still, I have a place to start."

"Show me," he said.

"And then?" she asked, trying and failing to keep the hope out of her voice.

"And then we'll see," he replied shortly, fearing that when what was going on in Madagascar became clear, someone would be ordered to kill her.

Imrich smiled and stepped up to kiss him, but Bolan put his hand out and stopped her short. "I said we'll see. Nothing more and no promises. I'll do what I have to do, and my mission—not yours and certainly not Rija's—comes first."

"Agreed," she said. "We'll eat something, rest, and then we'll head back into the city tonight."

BOLAN FOLLOWED DUSANA back down to the dining room, his thoughts tumbling over each other in rapid succession. He didn't know what to think. A part of him—a big part if he were honest with himself—wanted to help the woman. He knew the havoc that Velona was causing, and the temptation was always to remove problems, but removing one problem often brought greater ones and no real solution. The days of the kingmakers were over, and he knew from harsh experience that the world was far more delicately balanced than many people knew or would even believe.

Quite often, even the most justified coup, in humanitarian terms, might have very negative, far-reaching consequences elsewhere. And that didn't even count the cost in human lives at ground zero. It was the other costs: lost weapons sold on the black market, warlords seeking revenge, blood vendettas, world economic implications for oil, corn or other commodities…it was all tied together. One horrible, ugly system that everyone had to live with, or as was often the case, die with.

Working with Stony Man Farm meant making a difference, sometimes in big ways with missions that quite literally meant saving the world, but more often in smaller ways, by removing a threat before it became so large that highly visible government agencies had to get involved.

Imrich paused as they entered the dining room. "Where would you like to sit?" she asked. "Rija takes the far end, but it's a big table, so wherever you'd like."

Bolan moved to take a seat on one side, leaving Rija his traditional post. The dining room itself was beautiful. The floors alternated between handmade tile decorated with elaborate local patterns and hardwood. The walls were whitewashed stone, and decorated with a variety of paintings and tapestries.

On three sides, leaded glass allowed light to pour into the room and reflect off the polished wood surface of the table; it was clearly a room meant for entertaining guests. Freshly cut flowers were a burst of color in a crystal vase. "Isn't it lovely?" Dusana asked.

"Thank you," Rija said, entering the room through the main archway. "Dusana can claim credit for almost everything here in terms of the design, but the dining room is mine."

"I'm surprised," he said. "Not what I would expect from a militia general. This is warm and charming, the heart of a host. I expected a more traditional *Malagache* dining room with mats on the floor."

The general smiled at the compliment and took his seat. "Indeed, that is what was in my heart when I arranged for its appointments. I admit that I've been influenced by the comforts of Western culture. I take most of my meals with the men or in my office, but I prefer to eat here. Meals are a time for companionship and joy, not for business or serious talk."

"Agreed," Imrich said, her look offering Bolan a brief warning to follow Rija's lead.

"Agreed," the Executioner echoed, just as Maria entered the room with a tray.

"Ranonapango?" Bolan asked.

"Very good, Mr. Cooper. Some people do not appreciate the delicacy of our special rice drink, but nothing complements the flavor of the curry so well."

Maria returned to bring the parts of the main course to the table: fresh oysters on the half shell, fish curry served with several rice dishes and mounds of vegetables. There was separate chicken curry with flatbread and vegetable soup on the side.

"Amazing," Bolan complimented Maria.

"I told her you were coming," Imrich admitted. "I thought you might enjoy a traditional meal."

"It's mouthwatering," he said.

"Will there be anything else?" Maria asked.

"No, it's perfect, as always."

"Save a little room for dessert," she scolded in a teasing voice. "Our perfect fruit and vanilla ice cream is waiting for you."

"Fantastic," Rija said. "That, and coffee and perhaps an after-dinner drink, will make this a meal to remember."

Maria smiled, bowed and returned to the kitchen.

"Please, help yourselves," he said. "Among friends, formalities are often wasted."

Conversation was light and casual, interspersed between bites of the well-prepared food. Rija spoke about the building of the compound, while Imrich added tidbits about the security measures she'd managed to get into place while simultaneously keeping the main house more residential than military in feel.

When everyone had finished, Rija suggested they adjourn to the living room for an after-dinner drink. He poured a rich cognac into heavy crystal snifters and passed them around.

The room was filled with the golden glow of indirect lighting and heavy, white candles.

Imrich offered a toast, holding up her drink in salute. "To friends, new and old."

"Indeed," Rija said, raising his glass.

Bolan smiled, kept his silence and lifted his cognac.

Everyone had a sip and the dinner conversation turned to more serious matters. Bolan kept his thoughts to himself as he half listened to Imrich and Rija discuss the status of the men in the militia, continued improvements to the compound and other relatively benign topics.

He remained lost in his own thoughts until Imrich nudged him.

"What do you think, Cooper?" she asked, obviously repeating herself.

"About what?" he asked.

"We were discussing a personnel problem," Dusana said. "One of the men—Rija's second-in-command for the militia troops—was in 'Rivo recently."

"Why is that a problem?" he asked. "You don't let them go into the city?"

"He was spotted going into one of the buildings known to be under the control of Velona's secret police."

"Oh," Bolan said. "That is a problem. Do you have any more information?"

"Not just yet," Rija said. "We are waiting to hear back from some of…what is the word you use, Dusana?"

"Assets," she said.

"Yes, assets."

"You have been busy down here, haven't you?" Bolan asked.

"Just getting the system up and running," she replied.

"Are you training the men, too?" he asked. "Or leaving that to the military minds?"

"I've done some work with them," she said, hedging. "Nothing too fancy."

Uh-huh, he thought. "If I were advising you, I would say wait to deal with this man until you have more facts."

"Agreed, but there has been more than enough talk on this subject," Rija said, rising to his feet. "And now, I must bid you both good night. Tomorrow will be an early day for me, and I understand that you will both be going back into the city tonight?"

"That's the plan," Bolan replied, getting to his feet to return the short bow Rija offered. "I appreciate your gracious hospitality."

"Thank you for coming," Rija said. "Please do consider what Dusana has told you very seriously. The situation here in Madagascar is more perilous than your spy agencies know, and a humanitarian crisis is in no one's interest."

"We can agree on that much," Bolan said. "I'll think on all of it with due care."

"Good night, then," Rija said. "And good hunting."

The man was charming, in any event. He could see why Imrich liked him. Rija headed upstairs, leaving them to their own devices.

Bolan finished off his drink and returned the glass to the bar.

"Are you finished?" she asked. "Or would you like another?"

"I'm done," he said. "I've had more alcohol today than I normally have in a month."

"It doesn't mix well in our line of work," she said.

"No, it doesn't. Now what?"

"I was hoping we could talk some more," she said. "I want to know what you're thinking."

"I think your boss had it right—enough talk for one day." She started to protest, but he held up a hand, silencing her.

"I've heard what you have to say and I understand everything, okay? I just need to let it roll around in my mind for a bit."

"Fair enough," she said, running her hand up his arm. "Perhaps there's something else we can do?"

"Dusana…" he protested.

She walked out of the room and crooked her finger as she walked around the corner. When he didn't follow, she peeked back around. "I know exactly what you want."

Bolan quirked an eyebrow. Curious, he followed, cleared the corner and walked into Imrich as she pulled a pistol from the wall of weapons that was hidden in a closet. She pulled the slide back, chambering a round.

"I'm no fool, Cooper. I told you I know what you want. Let's go get your guy."

She reached behind the counter and pulled out his duffel bag, unzipping it as she dropped it onto the surface. "Shall you load or shall I?"

Bolan smiled. "You're my kind of girl."

10

His real name wasn't Smith, of course. Not that it mattered to him what name his current employer wanted to call him. He sat in the small café on the edge of the Independence Square, drinking Turkish coffee in spite of the heat. To passersby, he would be one anonymous face in the crowd—a tourist, possibly, or a businessman taking a break.

Smith had known men like Cooper all of his life, and his assessment of them was that they were usually long on action and short on thought. When the landing went badly, Smith had only one goal: escape into the city and disappear. Cooper took the fight to them, which in Smith's opinion, was a waste of time and a risk of life. He much preferred the life of the chameleon, the invisible assassin, to direct confrontation.

On the table in front of him was a satellite phone, and as he glanced at his watch to confirm the time back in the States, it rang. Right on schedule.

He answered it on the second ring. "This is Mr. Smith."

The familiar voice of Cecil Emritis, Secretary of the Interior, replied. "What's your status, Mr. Smith?"

"We landed in 'Rivo and barely got on the ground before a hostile force took out the plane and almost killed us both," he said. "Looked like some local militia rather than government forces."

"And Cooper?"

"We got separated during the fight," Smith said. "Last I saw, he jumped in a jeep with some dark-haired woman and took off."

"A woman?" Emritis asked. "Local?"

"I don't know," he said. "Probably. He mentioned having some resources here."

"And the secretary?"

"Not certain yet. Intel has him with a local militia group and this so-called general, Rija, has claimed responsibility, but I don't buy it. As of right now, I don't have a lock on the secretary's location."

"Well, get one, damn it! The longer he's missing the more pressure there is to send in a whole team with or without the sanction of the Madagascar government. The President has faith that this Cooper guy can get the job done. I've never even heard of Matt Cooper, and no one else seems to know him, either. Do you think he's that good?"

Smith paused and considered the small amount of data he'd already gathered. Anyone who could get through the firefight they'd encountered at the airport had some skill, but Cooper had handled it with more ease than others. There was something different about his fighting style, and his confidence level was high. "I imagine he's pretty good," he answered.

"Well, if you're not better than him I'm not getting my money's worth."

He bristled at the skepticism. "Of course you'll get your money's worth, Mr. Secretary."

"See that I do. Get this done. Next time we talk I want progress not excuses. I'll call for an update in twenty-four hours, Smith. And remember, I don't want Cooper or the secretary to ever be seen or heard from again. Is that understood?"

"Crystal clear," Smith replied, then he disconnected the call.

THE CAPITAL CITY OF MADAGASCAR was Antananarivo, or 'Rivo as it was more commonly called, and it boasted a population of more than a million souls. It was an old city, going back to the early 1600s, and in spite of some efforts at remodeling and modernizing, there were still many urban slums where people lived in abject poverty, surrounded by crime and with few contemporary comforts. Poor sanitation and infectious diseases were common, and Bolan knew from other missions that many young women were sold into near-slavery or the sex trade. Unless you belonged to the moneyed few or were part of the government, life in 'Rivo was dangerous and harsh.

Bolan and Imrich arrived in one of the outlying warehouse districts about an hour after sunset. In the distance, the lights from Independence Square glowed yellow and orange, giving tourists and panhandlers a false sense of protection from the shadows that closed in after dark. Imrich parked the jeep on a side street and shut down the engine.

"Where are we?" Bolan asked, pitching his voice low.

"There's a warehouse two blocks from here that I think we should explore. It's been used as a holding facility for some of the other militias and gangs in the area. Kidnapping for ransom is almost as big a trade as illegal drugs and prostitutes here."

"What kind of security will it have?" he asked, checking to ensure that his Desert Eagle was loaded, and that he had his usual assortment of backup weapons and ammunition in place.

"It's hard to say," she replied, going through her own prebattle ritual. "No one owns the place, really, so whoever is using it at any given time might change things up. We'll just have to improvise."

"Is there any chance the Secretary of State is in there?"

She shook her head. "It's doubtful. He's too high-value. My hope is we'll find someone to beat some information out of."

Bolan climbed out of the jeep and Imrich followed suit. "Sounds like a plan to me," he said. "Let's go."

They moved through the street covering each other like a well-oiled machine. Teaming up with Imrich may not always be simple, but he knew that her prowess in the field made her an incredible asset. They reached the warehouse, circled to a broken window and slipped inside. The building looked abandoned, crates in varying states of wear, along with blackened marks that licked up the walls, showed the chaos that often occupied the area. They moved through the debris and up to the second level of offices with no interruption.

Bolan lowered his pistol and turned to Imrich. "It doesn't look like this has been used for a while."

"The assault that caused the fire must have put a damper on the activities in the area. Have no fear. If there is anything that 'Rivo has to offer, it's shady places with thugs."

Glass crunched under Bolan's boots as he moved to the broken window to survey the landscape. The lights of the neighborhood turned from a few distant spots of light to lines of vehicles moving in on the warehouse.

"We've got company," he said. The first truck passed beneath one of the rare working streetlamps. "Government, it looks like."

Imrich ran to the corner to check the other windows. "They're coming…all sides. How the hell did they even know we were here?"

"That's a great question that we can find the answer to later," Bolan said. "Right now, we have to get the hell out of here." He scanned the cluttered warehouse for a likely exit aside from the door they'd used to come in. "Is there a side entrance?"

"This way," she said, moving into a light jog and slipping between the stacked debris like a cat.

Bolan followed in her wake, trying to listen and pinpoint where the government vehicles were stopping. A loudspeaker crackled as it came to life and the broken windows lit up as spotlights were trained on the building.

"Le bâtiment est entouré! Venez dehors et jetez vos armes au sol!" a voice demanded.

"Unless he's lying, they've got men on all sides," Imrich whispered as she stopped in front a small side door. "Got any ideas?"

"This was supposed to be a stealth mission," Bolan said. "What's on the other side of the door?"

"It's a pretty narrow alley, but about half a block down, there's a passage to the next warehouse."

Bolan moved to the door and tried to listen, but the man on the loudspeaker repeated his demand for them to come out and drop their weapons on the ground. He sighed. "It's lousy, but I don't think we have much choice. It's make a break for it or surrender."

She nodded. "I'll go first, and you cover. Left and right sides. If we don't stop, we might make it."

Bolan grinned. Imrich never backed down from a fight. "Try not to kill anyone," he said. "We just need to get out of here, and if we start killing government soldiers they'll be out in force and won't stop hunting us until we're run to ground."

"I'll be good," she said, turning the door handle, which creaked with alarming volume in the rafters of the warehouse. "Ready?"

"As ever," he said. "Go!"

She hit the door with her shoulder, sending it flying open, then dived across the alley in a long roll. It was thankfully dark, but the noise had attracted attention and men were moving in from the front side of the building already. She came up with a 9 mm pistol in each hand, pulling the triggers fast enough to send the men scrabbling for cover.

Bolan slipped out of the door, checked the back side, and said, "Let's move!"

They began moving down the alleyway, Imrich on the left, covering their front, and Bolan on the right, covering the back. Between their efforts and the lack of light, they managed to move down to the passage while laying down enough covering fire to keep both ends of the alley clear.

A side door burst open and two heavily armed government gunners burst through it, blocking their escape. Bolan and Imrich dropped their guns to the deck. The two men were straight out of an action movie, looking more like bodybuilders than soldiers and sporting matching tattoos on their forearms.

"Interesting ink they have there. What are those, bulls?"

"Yeah," Imrich said. "The symbol for their version of special forces."

They chatted idly, each time they spoke making small movements backward trying to create some space between them and the hulking giants before them.

"It's odd, though." Imrich stared. "The one on the left there, the horns of his bull are full of notches."

"Is that kind of like notches on a gun belt?"

"Kind of the same deal," she said.

"Well, I'd like to stay off of his list," Bolan said.

The two soldiers began to advance, closing the small gap that Bolan and Imrich created. The larger one with the notches pulled out a wicked-looking blade that the Executioner would have called an Arkansas toothpick if it weren't curved, and tossed it between his hands. The look on his face was less anger and more friendly menace.

"He's mine," Bolan said.

Imrich grabbed his arm. "Ladies first," she said. "I insist."

Bolan swept his arm forward gallantly. "Go for it."

Imrich moved next to Bolan and closed the distance between her and the brute. Pushing off her companion, she charged forward. The attack surprised her adversary and he swung out with the blade. She ducked, springing forward as she did, landing behind him and in front of the second man. Mr. Notches spun to see where she landed. Imrich kicked the knife out of his hand, sending it flying into the air. The second man was on Imrich and tried tossing her into the wall. She kicked her feet out just in time to grab traction on the wall and threw herself over his shoulder, crashing into the ground, winded but alive.

Bolan charged in with the knife from the thug in hand and made quick work of the second guy, driving the blade into his throat before turning his attention to the man who was trying to make mincemeat out of Imrich. Bolan tapped the man on the shoulder. When the guy glanced up, Bolan's fist connected with his jaw, knocking him out cold.

"You all right?" he asked her.

"Yeah, but I could have handled it," she said.

"I know, but it never hurts to improve your odds."

"Well, let's improve them considerably and get the hell out of here."

The building was swarming with troops, and their exits were getting fewer. Bolan and Imrich continued to move down the alley hugging the wall.

"Almost there," she said, dumping an empty magazine and popping in a new one in a single, smooth, motion.

Bolan cranked several more rounds in the general direction of the soldiers, forcing them into cover once more, then turned and saw the passage. Imrich was just stepping into it when he saw the shadowy form of a man behind her.

He didn't stop to think, didn't wonder what to do, he simply leaped forward and knocked her out of the way as the man raised his gun to shoot. There was the briefest flash of light from the muzzle, but it was enough for him to see the man's face.

The first round buzzed past Bolan's ear, but the next one, a split second later, hit with a roar, a burst of burning pain, and then nothing as the big American went down.

11

He knew that the sounds he was hearing were supposed to be words, but for what seemed like a long time, they were blurred and fuzzy. It sounded as if someone was speaking to him underwater. He was determined to rise, and he floated toward consciousness. The awareness of impending death took him full-on, startling him into wakefulness.

Bolan shook his head to clear the remaining cobwebs and immediately regretted it as a lance of pain shot through his skull. On the other hand, the pain helped. The cobwebs were gone.

"Don't do that, Cooper," Imrich said. "You're going to have a hell of a headache for a day or two."

He blinked his eyes, doing his best to ignore his throbbing skull. "I thought you were dead," he said, startled at how weak his voice came out. "Or maybe me."

"I got lucky," she said, then paused. "We got lucky, Matt. You because you have the luck of the Devil himself sometimes, and me because I had you. You saved me."

"Someone shot me," he remembered. "I pushed you out of the way."

"You did," Imrich replied. "And thanks."

He thought back and said, "That guy Smith was there. He tried to kill us both." Angered, he began to sit up, then eased back when the room decided to take a long, slow spin around him. "Damn. I wondered about that guy. Should've trusted my instincts and killed him on the plane before we ever landed." He held out his hand. "Help me up."

Imrich grabbed his hand, and he held tight, taking several deep breaths until the dizziness passed. I'll live, he thought, scanning the room as he realized that he was in a hospital bed and Imrich was wearing blue nurse's scrubs. "How did I get here?"

"The government security forces brought you in. They had an ambulance in tow, so they loaded you right up. So far, they don't know your identity, but they're working hard and fast on it. From what I was able to overhear on my way in, they want to prove you were sent by the U.S. government. It will give them a reason to stir up a real international incident and give them some coverage on the matter of the Secretary of State." She shuddered. "I hate politics."

"That makes two of us," he said. "You, I take it, are my Florence Nightingale?"

"It got me in here, yeah," she replied. "But now the trick is getting back out."

"How long have I been unconscious?"

She consulted her watch. "A few hours. They bandaged you up, but there wasn't much else to do." She grinned. "It was barely a scratch, you know. Head wounds bleed a lot."

"Funny. It doesn't feel like a scratch," he said. "Have any thoughts on what we might do next?"

"First order of business is getting you out of here before they realize that you've woken up. So far the media is on lockdown, but I heard a couple of the soldiers talking in the hall. If they identify you as American, the plan is to go public immediately. They've been here three times looking to question you, and they keep asking me the same things."

"How did you get out?"

She smiled. "Stripped down to my black tank and shorts

and played wounded girl. I told them that you were holding me hostage."

"Thanks," Bolan said. "Where's my stuff?"

Imrich crossed the room and double-checked the hall, then came back. "Just so you know, there are two guards posted outside the door. They're looking pretty bored right now, but the second they think you're awake they'll be in here. Do this quietly."

She opened the small wardrobe that was built into the wall and removed his clothes. The shirt was splattered with droplets of blood. "Great," she said quietly. "This will be inconspicuous."

He realized that she was staring at him and said, "What?"

"Not very modest, are you?"

Bolan suddenly realized that he was standing in front of her with barely a stitch of clothing on. "You could have turned around," he suggested. "But it's not like you haven't seen it all before."

She was silent for a moment, then laughed. "Maybe, but you don't turn away from a beautiful work of art *that* easily. I'm weak that way where you're concerned."

Bolan finished tucking in the shirt, trying to hide most of the blood. "All set."

Imrich turned back from peeking out the door. "Good enough. We'll get you some other clothes later. Right now…" Her voice trailed off as she gazed at the door again. She reached underneath the small nightstand next to the bed. "Here," she said, handing his guns to him. "You're going to need these again. Sooner, rather than later, I'm guessing. I already checked the loads."

"Thanks," he said. "I wondered if they were gone." He slid the Desert Eagle into its hip holster and the Glock into his waistband at the small of his back, then put on his jacket.

"All right," she said. "Here's what I figure. The government will keep the media locked down for as long as they can with Secretary of State's kidnapping. That's another twelve, maybe twenty-four hours at most. They are going to be beating every tree in the jungle looking for him or whoever they think did it. I'm guessing their spies in the city outed us at the warehouse in the first place. Plus, now they think they have an American spy to look for. Am I right so far?"

"Yes," he said. "So, we need to get out of here, get the secretary back, find out what in the hell Smith is up to and neutralize him. We've probably got twenty-four hours before the Madagascar government confronts the U.S. to say they had a suspected spy in custody and demand some answers. They'll want to get me first."

"Perfect," Imrich said. "This isn't the newest *Mission Impossible* film. You know that, right?"

"I don't pick the mission, Dusana, it picks me, but Murphy's Law seems to be in full effect for this one. First the attack at the airport and then the ambush at the building."

"So, we've got twenty-four hours to complete your goals. Where do we start?"

"I've got an idea," he said with a meaningful look at the door. "If you're willing. Worst case, we can always shoot our way out."

"Let's hear it," she said. "The sooner we're out of here, the sooner I can prove to you that we're on your side. Don't forget why I'm helping you."

Bolan paused at the reminder of her cause. He slipped the pistol out of its holster and rechecked the ammo before locking it back in place. He didn't really need the reminder that she was already walking a slippery slope and taking him along the edge of it with her.

"I never forget anything, Dusana. Now, let's get the hell out of here."

Bolan stuffed the bed with pillows from the closet and

covered them with blankets. The right amount of tucking and drawing the curtains against the light that was barely beginning to ease over the horizon made the form more believable.

"That's your plan?" she asked.

"You got a better one?"

She paused, and Bolan could see the thoughts creeping around in her head before she looked at him squarely. "No."

"Good. Now, you get their attention and keep their eyes off the fire exit. I'll meet you one level down."

"I sure hope this works."

"Me, too. My head is still killing me, and the idea of shooting before the drumbeats in my head stop doesn't sound very appealing."

Bolan waved her forward and watched from behind the door as she slipped past him and into the hallway, leaving it open just a crack behind her. One of the guards quickly asked if he was awake and she told him no, but that she had some information that might be interesting.

Imrich moved several steps down the hallway and both guards followed, anxious to hear what she had to say. Bolan watched them eye her backside, as interested in that as what she might have to say. They turned away from his door, just as planned. He crept silently out behind them and moved rapidly down the hallway, crossing into the fire exit stairwell.

He followed the stairs down one floor, then waited several minutes, keeping an eye on the hallway. He'd begun moving toward the elevators when two security guards in government uniforms came around the far corner. Bolan ducked into an employee changing room that was fortunately empty. Snaring a lab coat from a wall hook and donning it, he peered out the door.

The two guards were gone. He added a clipboard to his disguise, and then moved to the elevators, staring at the notes in front of him until the doors opened. Imrich was inside, waiting for him.

"Buy you a cup of coffee in the cafeteria?" she quipped.

"Sure thing," he said, stepping into the car. "So long as you mean a cafeteria far, far from here."

"I do," she said, pushing the button for the ground floor. "Any problems?"

She shook her head. "No, they peeked inside the room, but didn't check any closer. Our dummy under the blankets worked for the moment, though I imagine that the next time a nurse comes to check on you they'll figure it out."

He opened his mouth to ask how long she thought that might be when a building alarm started shrieking at full volume.

She looked at him, the amusement plain on her face. "About now, I'd say."

"I guess it's still working," he muttered.

"What's that?"

"Murphy's Law," he said. "I guess we'll be leaving the hard way."

"Probably," she said. "Can you fight?"

"Do I have a choice?"

She offered a lopsided grin. "Probably not," she said.

"Then I can fight," he said.

The little floor lights above the elevator door flashed in sequence: 3, 2, 1, and then with a slight shudder, G. "Get ready," she said. "The information desk is straight across from us, and the exit doors are on our right."

"Let's try not to kill any civilians," Bolan said. "The situation's bad enough. No need to make it worse."

"Agreed," she said, as a soft bell sounded and the doors opened onto the main floor of the hospital.

They stepped out of the elevator car, moving in a wide arc to the right. The building alarm was still sounding and nurses flittered about like bees while the hospital security staff had bunched up by the front exit. Their shoulder-mounted radios were squawking as the guards from the floor he'd been on gave his description.

Bolan took them in with a quick glance, realizing that these weren't the normal hospital security people, but government soldiers.

"Here we go," Imrich whispered at his shoulder.

As the radio transmission ended, the nearest guard looked up and his eyes went wide. He tried to point and reach for his gun at the same time, while shouting, "There he is!"

Bolan had the Glock free from beneath his coat, aimed and fired before the other three guards at the door could figure out what was going on. His frangible round hit the guard in the left eye, the force of it knocking him backward with a pained grunt. The bullet shattered on impact, pieces lodging in his brain and killing him instantly.

Imrich had her own weapon free, and she rolled forward, amazingly agile. Her first shot took one guard in the stomach, doubling him over, with a horrified expression on his face. Blood spattered onto the tile floor, a bright crimson splash on pale green.

They both fired, almost simultaneously, as the last two guards opened up with their assault rifles. Bullets sprayed the floor and ceiling, ricocheting off the hard tile as Bolan cut to his left and fired to his right in the same movement, doing his best not to trip over Imrich, who had regained her feet and popped up like a jack-in-the-box straight from hell.

Her shot took a guard beneath the chin, while his was center mass. Both guards dropped, their weapons clattering to the floor.

His and Imrich's moves, Bolan realized, had been like a well-choreographed ballet, as though they knew what the other was going to do, when and how they would move.

Their eyes met a split second after the last guard fell. The building alarm still shrieked and, they could hear the sound of approaching sirens. Behind them, hospital employees screamed in terror from their hiding places.

"Time to go," she said, moving to the doors. "Quickly."

"No question on that," Bolan answered, stepping outside.

They reached the street as a familiar, rickety-looking cab slammed to a halt. The front passenger door shot open and Gabriel shouted, "Get in here, you damn fools, before you get me shot!"

Bolan looked a question at her, but she shrugged. His instincts told him Gabriel was here for a reason, and they may as well find out what it was. He ushered the woman into the cab and jumped in behind her.

"Go, Gabriel!" Imrich yelled.

"Gone," he replied, hitting the accelerator. On the dashboard, the Virgin Mary smiled back at them, as though blessing their escape.

12

Once they were well away from the hospital, Imrich gave Gabriel an address, then leaned back in the seat and sat silently next to Bolan. While the injury he'd suffered earlier wasn't serious, his head was still pounding, and while the adrenaline from their escape had made it possible for him to fight, that was quickly wearing off.

Gabriel stopped the cab next to a large storage facility. "Here you go," he said, eyeing them both in the mirror. "You two look like hell."

"Feel like it, too," Imrich said, stepping out of the cab. Bolan followed her, but paused as another wave of nausea rolled in his stomach. The pain in his head arced across his skull and took up residence behind his left eye. He took several deep breaths, swallowing hard, and forced it back down. There was something about getting a graze on the head that could take the starch right out of a man. What he needed was some rest and to give his body a few hours to recover.

Imrich watched him carefully for a moment, and when he nodded, she guided him to a large storage unit. She unlocked it and slid the doors back, revealing a fully decked out Humvee. "With any luck, we can retrieve the other vehicle later, but right now, I think it's best if we just get out of the city."

Doing his best to swallow his nausea, Bolan nodded once more, then made his way over to the Humvee and climbed inside. Once he'd shut the door, he leaned back against the headrest and wondered if the pain behind his eye was ever going to go away.

"We'll get back to the compound where it's safe and get you fixed up," Imrich said.

Bolan couldn't tell her he didn't feel any safer there than in the hospital, but for now the location wasn't up to him, so it would have to do. The roads into the jungle were unforgiving, and every bump sent a new and sensational pain through his head. Imrich stopped the vehicle and pulled a med kit from under the seat.

"Here, take this," she said, handing him a foil packet. Inside was a tablet.

"What is it?"

"Do you really care, Cooper?" she asked pointedly. "I'm not going to poison you, but if you want your head to stop hurting so bad, that will help."

She was absolutely right. It didn't matter at this point. If she wanted him dead she could have done that easily enough before now. Bolan popped the tablet into his mouth as Imrich put the truck in gear and continued down the road. It wasn't long before the pain began to subside and the medicine was wooing him to sleep.

BOLAN WOKE WHEN Imrich honked the horn, opening the main gate to the compound. The pain in his head was reduced to an annoying thrum that was much more manageable.

"Welcome back," Imrich said. "How are you feeling?"

He eased himself fully upright. "Better, thanks."

They parked the Humvee and walked into the main house, which was blessedly cool and quiet. "I could use some food and coffee," he said. "And I also need a phone. A secure one, if you have it."

"Of course," she said. "I could eat, too, but I need to talk with Rija first. Just use the same room as before—the phone line is secure, and I'll send Maria in with some food." She eyed him critically. "Are you sure you don't want to rest a bit more first?"

Bolan gave her a hard stare for several beats.

"Forget I asked!" she said. "Go do what you've got to do. All the phone lines in the compound are secure. I have to check in with Rija and give him an update. Things did not go as planned, so he's likely to be unhappy. It could take me a while."

"That's fine," he said. "We can catch up later." He watched as she headed toward Rija's office, then he turned and moved up the stairs to the bedroom suite they'd used before. There was a small desk, phone, and access ports for connecting a laptop to the compound network. He sat down in the comfortable desk chair and rubbed his temples for a moment, mentally adding the need for a shower to his list of things to get done in short order.

Bolan pulled his phone out of his pocket and plugged the phone line into the device on one end and the phone on the other. Before dialing, he ran a quick program that swept the room for other transmission devices. As he'd expected, there were bugs in several places. Another key sent out a short scrambler code that would jam their signal as well as anyone trying to listen in on the phone line. Using the landline would mark his location for Brognola, which might be important if things got any worse.

He dialed the special number for the big Fed's desk, and the phone was picked up almost immediately. "Striker? It's about damn time I heard from you, considering that your last known location was the plane getting blown to pieces when it landed."

"I'm not dead yet, Hal," he said. "But it's not for a lack of people trying. And the Secretary of the Interior's man, Smith, was a plant. He disappeared after we landed and got into that firefight, but then last night, he tried to kill us."

"Us?"

"I've been working with Dusana Imrich on the ground," he said. "You remember her."

Brognola sighed into the phone. "Striker, you never fail to find a complicated situation, do you? I can't believe that Smith…tell me you're joking."

"Wish I were. I got a nice graze across my skull for the trouble. Do you think the SoI is in on all this somehow?"

"Smith was his man, so he must be, but I don't know what his game is. I'll look into it on this end. But listen, the President is getting more and more nervous. The government there knows we've got someone on the ground and they're just aching for a chance to prove it. He's ready to send in a team if this goes on much longer. Do you have any leads?"

"Dusana introduced me to this General Rija, and I'm at his compound now. He told me that their claim of involvement was all smoke and mirrors. I think he's trying to make a name for himself and get a seat at the big boy's table. He acts like he's a Good Samaritan, and Dusana says he's on the right side of things."

"Listen, Striker, Rija does a good job with his man of the people act, but that's just what it is. An act. The man the media has been seeing isn't the same one as the people in the villages get to meet. I'm sending you a video file right now."

Bolan began streaming it on his phone as it arrived. The video was poor quality and obviously shot from some distance, but there was no doubt that the man giving the orders to the execution squad was Rija. Worse, he laughed as he watched his men rape a woman in a crude demonstration of their power. The nausea was back, but this time it didn't have anything to do with the injury to his skull.

"I can see he's a charmer," Bolan said. "I guess I should've known better. Where did we get this video?"

"One of our local informants sent it yesterday," Brognola said. "It's verified as unaltered." He paused, then added, "Our informant says Rija has the Secretary of State, Striker. He's involved."

"I guess it's convenient I'm here. I can take care of Rija right now."

"Easy, Striker, I know how you feel, but the SoS is and must be our mission priority. We can deal with Rija's sins later. I highly doubt he has him there. Remember this is a guy who has two faces. He'll have one place where he can invite the media and world leaders, and another that will be something less sophisticated. Until you figure out where the SoS is, and how to get him out, you're going to have to play it cool."

"How long do I have?"

"In less than twenty-four hours the U.S. sends in a strike team. One is being prepped as we speak."

"Who's leading it?"

"Major Walt Ketchum."

"He's quite the hard-ass. Hopefully we'll be long gone before he has to deploy."

"Good luck, Striker. And remember, that team will be on the move and ready to hit the coast by the time the twenty-four-hour clock is up. Don't be late."

"I believe in being punctual, Hal. I'll get him out."

Bolan hung up and paced the room. Rija. There were few things that could make his blood boil quicker than a despot hurting the people around him, but a two-faced one who was attempting to tie Bolan to his endeavors sent him over the edge.

He pulled his phone out of the phone jack and continued to pace. He punched a code on his phone and looked for a camera system but couldn't find one in the room. If Rija was involved, then it stood to reason that Imrich was involved, but there was a nagging voice in the back of his head that contradicted that notion.

Bolan slid the phone under the door and tapped into the camera system in the hallway. Using the same jamming frequency as he had on the bugs, he disabled the cameras' recording function. Until he shut it off, the image would remain static. The phone displayed a 3D map of all the areas he'd already been to and what a low-orbit satellite could provide. The troop movements outside were precise, but nothing showed that any area was more heavily guarded than another.

He moved through the hallway, mapping as he went and searching for heat signatures of guards in each area. Movements were noted and added to the overlay of the compound. Bolan moved to the second level and worked through each room. The end of the second floor hallway was a locked steel door. The security lock could be opened with a key, and lucky for Bolan his phone was the ultimate electronic key. A clear plastic card ejected from the end of the phone, and the soldier inserted it into the key slot.

The bolts for the door slid open and Bolan crept inside. The room was filled with weapons and explosives. He gave a low whistle as he looked at the arsenal. Moving to the control keypad that was behind the lock, he saw a small display that rotated through the rooms of the compound. Imrich was leaving her meeting with Rija and heading back toward her room. He needed to be there when she returned.

Bolan exited the small armory and ran back to the room, careful to avoid any sentries in the hallway. He made it inside and released the bugs and hall cameras moments before she arrived. The door shut behind her just as he slipped the phone into his pocket. "How did your meeting with Rija go?" he asked, doing his best to keep the contempt out of his voice, to hide his anger at being deceived.

"About as expected," she said. "He's not happy. How was your call?"

"About as expected," he parroted.

He watched her as she moved about the room, pulling out a change of clothes and grabbing a towel. She noticed how he stared at her and stopped in her tracks.

"What?" she asked.

"I…"

Bolan knew he couldn't have this conversation here. He knew they needed to talk, and if she wasn't cooperative, he might even be forced to take steps. Bolan didn't want to do that, but Imrich was in the game, for better or worse, and that meant he had to treat her as a player, not just a partner or friend.

"I have to go back to the city," he said.

"What on earth for? You're not even close to being healed and you need rest."

"You know how it is. Orders are orders. I have business."

"Okay, just let me shower and put on clean clothes and we can go."

"You'll go with me?" he asked.

"Of course. I still have a job to do, too," she said, disappearing into the bathroom.

"I bet you do," he muttered.

13

"So what's the plan?" Imrich asked, sitting in the passenger seat and letting Bolan drive for the first time since they'd gotten together.

"I have an asset that needs to be interrogated."

"Where?"

"I thought we'd head back to the first warehouse we explored," the soldier stated.

"Do you think that's a good idea? The only thing we managed to accomplish the last time was to nearly get killed."

"That's why we'll go there now—no one will think to look for us there."

"Sounds reasonable enough," she said, then laughed. "Though you and reasonable don't often wind up on the same street."

Bolan circled the neighborhood that the warehouse was in and then brought the Humvee to rest just outside the alley where Smith had tried to take them out before. The Executioner stepped out of the vehicle and waited for his companion to walk around the side.

Imrich stepped into the warehouse in front of Bolan, and he moved in behind her, letting her hair spill through his fingers like a river of jet as he exposed her neck. Stepping close, he wrapped one arm around her waist, pulling her in tightly.

"If you wanted this kind of play, Cooper, we could have

stayed at the compound where there is a nice warm bed, good food and—"

As Bolan pulled a small cloth covered in chloroform out of his pocket and covered her mouth, the rest of her sentence was cut off. She struggled against him wildly for several long seconds, then went under and he lowered her to the ground. He removed the cloth the moment she went down, not wanting to dose her too strongly, and tossed it aside along with the glove that protected his hand from the noxious chemical.

He disarmed her and tossed her over his shoulder before dropping her into a battered-looking chair. He needed to work quickly before she regained consciousness. He grabbed some heavy twine lying on the floor and tied her feet together and then her hands, securing her to a pipe sticking out from the sheet metal wall. Bolan carefully removed any objects from the wall that might become a weapon, the last being a six-inch nail.

Her eyes fluttered opened, then went to half-mast—the cold, hungry stare of a predator cat. "If this isn't some weird kind of foreplay, you'd better start explaining yourself, Cooper. In fact, no matter what it is, you'd best start talking."

Bolan ignored her, pulling up a crate that appeared solid and taking a seat. He removed a long, thin-bladed knife from his boot, examined it for a moment, then sent it spinning her way. It hit the wall to the left of her eye, missing her by scant inches. He stood up and retrieved it, then sat back down. "If I don't get the right answers, Dusana, all the talking in the world won't save you again. All I've done since I got here was talk and get dragged from one trap to another. I'm out of patience."

"You're not—"

"So now you're going to tell me, Dusana, where the Secretary of State is being held. You do that, give me what I need to know, and you live to fight another day. I'll even give you a twenty-four-hour head start, because when I've finished this mission, I *will* come looking for you. But for now, give me the information and we can end this particular game of cat and mouse with you still alive."

She stared at him and then shook her head. Bolan could see the remnants of the drug working their way out of her system. "Cooper, this is crazy. What in the hell are you talking about? I've been trying to help you! I didn't purposely lead you into a trap. As you recall, they weren't exactly shooting blanks at me in the hospital or in the warehouse."

"I understand that. That's why we're talking and not doing anything more…proactive for the moment. How much do you really know about Rija's activities?"

"Everything," she said. "I haven't hidden anything from you. I've told you everything."

"You see, that's the problem, Dusana. You haven't. You do know he's just another warlord, right? Beating and killing and raping because no one can stop him?"

"Cooper, you have him all wrong. Anything like that is rumor, and he doesn't dissuade it because it keeps his reputation going. Just like the ploy to take the credit for the secretary."

"Yeah, I've heard the 'ploy' story already," he said. "The problem is, I don't believe it."

She paused and took a deep breath. "Cooper, I assume I wouldn't be trussed up like Christmas turkey if you were merely speculating. What do you have?"

Bolan pulled up the video that Brognola sent him of Rija's atrocities. He held it up for Imrich to watch. As she stared at the small screen, her eyes widened and her face grew pale. When she started to turn away, he snapped, "Watch it!"

Bolan knew the woman was trained well, but the horror on her face was something he'd never seen before. The screams of the woman being gang-raped filled the emptiness of the room, but she didn't turn away again. She knew the horrors of war. Knew what happened to family and friends. To children and innocents. He could never believe that she would exist in the same space as that kind of evil.

She stared up at him with unshed tears in her eyes and then quickly turned to the side and lost all of the contents of her stomach.

Bolan waited in the silence and then used the knife to cut the twine on her hands and feet. Imrich staggered to the stack of crates and collapsed on top of them, staring numbly at him.

"You didn't know?"

"I didn't know."

There was a long pause. Bolan heard a car pull up outside, and he stood and glared at her. She held up her hand. "Relax, it's Gabriel. I inform him every time I come into the city."

They heard Gabriel stumbling through a pile of rubble before he came into their corner of the warehouse. He paused and cocked an eyebrow when he saw the two of them looking so tense.

"You two all right?"

"No, well, I mean, yeah," Imrich said.

"Is Gabriel a part of Rija's party?"

"No," she said. "Rija never liked him. Gabriel is one of the best assets I have and he's mine alone. I don't share him."

"Umm…technically, that's not entirely true," Gabriel said.

"What do you mean?" she snapped.

"Here, I am your asset, but I also provide necessary information to…interested parties from overseas," he admitted. "After I saw what Rija was really up to, I had to act—even if it meant going against you."

"What are you talking about?" she asked.

Bolan showed Gabriel the video, and after a minute, he nodded. "Yes, I was the one who took that." He sat down next to Imrich. "I do not believe you knew or that you would have helped that monster."

"Thank you," she said. She turned to Bolan. "I hope you can believe that, too."

He sighed and nodded. "I do. Listen, is there *any* possibility that Rija has the secretary stashed away in the compound somewhere?"

"No way," she said. "I… He's obviously a very good manipulator, but that building is my baby. I know every inch of it and there isn't so much as a root cellar that I don't see at least once a week." She paused. "It's… I'm not denying he's a black hat, Cooper. Not at all. But how do you know he has the secretary? I would've known."

The frustration in her voice was easy to hear, and Bolan looked at Gabriel for an answer.

He nodded. "I saw what happened at the airport, and even tried to help after he left with his men. I don't know where he took him, but I don't doubt he has the secretary. I couldn't say anything to you, Dusana, until I was certain you weren't involved."

"I understand," she said. "But that still leaves us trying to find where Rija has hidden him. If he's not at the compound, I'm not even sure where to start."

Pacing back and forth, Bolan tried to think. Finally he said, "We're running out of time before this whole situation gets worse."

"They'll send in a team?" Imrich asked.

Bolan nodded. "Look, Rija isn't the mission. Help me get the secretary and then you can do whatever you want to him. I'll even help. Do you have any idea where he might be being held?"

Gabriel tentatively raised his hand. "I think I do. I had to take a group of men out for Rija once when Dusana wasn't here. I'm happy to serve the cause, so I saw no harm. There is an old fortress from the time of French occupation deep in the jungle."

"Can you remember how to get there?"

"Yes."

"Can you show me on a map?"

"No, too many twists and turns, but I memorized every turn of the road because I thought that, if I didn't, I would lose my way home and Dusana would be sending my bleached skull to my brother."

Through the open window came the sound of sirens and tires screeching to a halt on the hot asphalt. Bolan looked through the window and said, "Smith. The man's like a bad penny. Let's move."

Imrich quickly strapped on her shoulder holster, while Bolan and Gabriel gathered up their gear and put it in their duffel bags.

From his perch by the window, Gabriel said, "They're coming in. We've got maybe three or four minutes."

Bolan grabbed his bag and slung it over one shoulder. "Gabriel, they won't be looking for you. Go and hide on a different floor. Dusana, east stairs. I'll take the west." He started moving for the door, but Imrich grabbed his arm.

"We're splitting up?" she asked. "Why?"

"Better chance that one of us will escape and be able to finish the mission." He pulled his arm out of her grasp. "I'm sorry. I had to know."

Gabriel was already out the door and headed for the clunky stairs.

As she ducked out the door to the east he said, "On the way here I saw a statue of a guy with horses two blocks over and four blocks to the east in a park. We meet there when we're clear."

He didn't wait for her to answer, but instead ran for the

stairway, moving through the door and onto the damp and foul-smelling landing, his bag riding comfortably on his back.

Ten flights down he could hear the sounds of Smith's men starting up the stairs, banging and shouting as they came. He'd obviously cozied up to the government or the secret police to get the resources he needed.

Silently Bolan went down toward the noise, taking the stairs two and three at a time, glad to be out of the smell. He had to get lower into the building before he would have any chance at all of escaping without a major gun battle. Better to just get away without anyone knowing it and let Smith waste time looking for them.

He reached the fourth floor at the same moment as the sounds told him that the men below were passing the third. Pulling his gun, he ducked into the hallway and quickly and silently pulled the door closed behind him.

But for the moment his luck held. They pounded past the fourth floor and headed upward like a mad herd of wild beasts. He counted six men going up. And no sounds of fighting from the other side of the building, so Imrich had so far managed to avoid them, as well.

He waited until Smith's men were two floors above, then eased through the door and back out into the stairway. For the moment it was empty, but no doubt Smith would leave men stationed at the bottom of both stairwells.

He headed down, letting the sound of the men above him cover any noise he might make.

The guard at the bottom of the stairs had his back to him and was trying to light a thin cigar, not looking up. Clearly he was thinking that since the men had just gone upward, he had the easy duty. He was dead wrong as the Executioner slit the guard's throat and shoved his body aside.

The bottom of the stairwell had two doors, one into the warehouse and one leading out the side. A quick peek out

of the side door told Bolan that the alley on that side of the
building had two guards, both facing the street not more than
twenty steps from his position.

He eased out and into the shadows along the brick wall,
moving away from the front of the building. When both
guards were completely turned away, he crossed the alley
and reached a side door into another building. The air in
the alley was still hot from the day and the smell of rotting
food scattered in piles around a rusted can almost made his
eyes water.

Just as he reached the door he heard gunfire from the other
side of the warehouse. Clearly Imrich wasn't having it as easy
as he was at the moment.

Both the guards at the front of the alley reached for
their guns, so Bolan decided that Imrich might need a little
distraction. With single shots that seemed very loud in the
enclosed side alley, he dropped both guards face-forward
into the street.

Now that ought to keep them wondering what was going
on, he thought, and maybe give Imrich a little breathing room.

As shouting erupted from the front of the building, the
soldier slipped into the other building's side door and pulled
it closed behind him, locking it.

He found herself in the back service hallway of a restaurant.
Keeping his gun in his hand but holding it at his side, he went
through the restaurant kitchen, startling the half dozen people
who were working there. He nodded at the surprised chef and
said, "Smells wonderful," then rushed into the main area of
the restaurant, hiding his gun as he went.

The room had at least a dozen customers, all looking out
the window onto the street in front of the warehouse where
all of Smith's men were. He moved through the tables to a
door that opened onto the side street. Once outside, he put his
gun away and walked at a fast pace down the sidewalk, not

looking like he was in a hurry, yet moving quickly. Luckily, Smith hadn't thought to have guards stationed at the closest intersections.

The gunshots from the other side of the warehouse had stopped. He hoped that meant that Imrich had escaped and wasn't killed. She had mired herself into this mess, but Bolan felt guilty about this ambush and wanted to see them all get out alive.

Taking his time so as not to draw attention to himself, Bolan went through the dark side streets of 'Rivo, staying close to the buildings, avoiding groups of people as much as possible. The night air was thick and rich with the smells of many people cooking dinner. Every mission usually had one detail that stood out, something that he remembered. He had a hunch that this mission, if he survived, the thing he would remember would be the thick, rich smells of this city.

And the look on Rija's face when he killed him.

14

Bolan circled far around the park, easing into the grass and trees that occupied a half block on the side opposite the hotel. The statue he had seen out of the back of Gabriel's cab filled the center of the park, surrounded by a small stone courtyard.

He faded into the shadows of the copse and waited, leaning against the trunk of a large tree, not moving, trying to calm his breathing and just think. With luck, Gabriel had heard what he told Imrich about where to meet. If not, he was going to have to find him, and that wasn't going to be easy in a city this size.

On the west side of the park a figure crossed the street, hands in pockets, moving like she was out for an evening stroll and didn't have a care in the world. Imrich. The sight of her made him smile. It would take more than Smith and his goon squad to stop her. He almost felt sorry for Rija if she got to him before he did. Almost.

He pushed away from the rough bark of the tree and moved to meet her as she walked along the sidewalk on the outskirts of the park.

"Now where?" she asked, smiling as she approached.

"Find Gabriel," he said, returning her grin. He was relieved that she hadn't been involved in Rija's crimes. He would've been forced to take unpleasant measures. "Do you think he heard my instructions to come here?"

"I don't think so," Imrich said. "Too far down the hallway. And by the way, thanks for the distraction back at the warehouse. Kept half of them off my back."

"I figured it might work that way. So, got any ideas how we find one cab driver in a town this size?"

"You need to phone home again," Imrich said. "Gabriel was working for me, but many of my reports were couriered through him. He's an asset, and I bet your guys back home have alternate ways of finding him."

"Good idea." He glanced at the buildings they were walking past. Most of them had lights, but a few didn't. Clearly using the government's carrier had allowed Smith to trace Bolan's phone, so wherever they got the power needed for contacting Brognola, it needed to be a place easy to escape from and hard for Smith to attack. At least until the big Fed could lock out his satellite signal.

The area they were walking through consisted of mostly two-story buildings, clearly apartments that had seen better days.

Then he had an idea that might just prove to work double-duty for them. "From what I remember of the city plans, there's a bus terminal about ten blocks west of here."

Imrich nodded. "Not sure that would be the safest place to try to phone home."

"But from an apartment close to there it would be," he said.

She nodded. "I see. Smith will trace it and think we're stupid enough to try to get out of the city on a bus."

"Exactly," he said. "He'll spend a lot of manpower searching the terminal and the buses while we head south."

"Let's do it," she said, moving to step in beside him on the narrow sidewalk. "I like how you think."

"I think we need to split up again, just in case," Bolan said, suddenly realizing what an unusual sight they made walking along with their equipment bags. "I'll go south two blocks and down toward the bus terminal. You go north two blocks. We meet one block to the east of the terminal."

She nodded and without another word turned away from him at the intersection, staying in close to the buildings as she went.

FIFTEEN MINUTES LATER they were back together and inside a dark apartment on the lower floor of a two-story building a block from the bus terminal. The apartment had a window that would work well for their satellite link and it didn't look as if anyone had been home in a few days.

"This has got to be quick," Imrich said. "They will be ready to trace us this time."

"In and out," he said.

The phone pinged off the government satellite and Brognola picked up immediately.

"I wasn't expecting you to check back in so quickly."

"And it's going to have to be very quick," Bolan said. "Smith and his men have a way to track this signal. They rousted us out of our last location, and I have a feeling that's how we've ended up in so much trouble on this trip."

"Damn," Brognola said. "Are both you and Dusana all right?"

"No problem," Bolan said. "But we need three things. First, we need the contact information for Gabriel, a local cab driver who had been working with Dusana. He's been passing information along to the U.S., too, so he's probably in the database. He knows exactly where the compound is and is willing to take us there if we can find him again."

He heard the sound of Brognola typing furiously in the background, then he said, "Downloading it to you now."

"Second, we know that Rija's compound is about sixty-five miles south of the city in the jungle. It should be fairly easy to spot from space from my descriptions in my debriefing. I need all the intel on the area that you can get me."

"I'll get you everything I can and send it along."

"Understood," he said. "Third, we're going to need some better firepower if we're going at that compound. Can you give us a contact for an arms dealer in the city?"

"Hurry," Imrich said.

"I've finished downloading Gabriel's information and there's a weapons man in the city that should be reliable. I've sent his information along to your phone as well. Good luck."

"We're going to need it," Bolan said.

He downloaded Gabriel's information to a flash drive and handed it to Imrich. They had already decided they were going to split up again and where they would meet. They were out the door and moving in opposite directions away from the bus terminal thirty seconds later.

As Bolan walked, he pulled up Gabriel's information on his phone. Gabriel had been working with Imrich, he had had no reason to lie to his handler's headquarters, so Bolan figured the information was accurate.

But the question was, after separating from them, where would Gabriel go to try to find Imrich and Bolan? He wouldn't just go home, and he wouldn't just go back to driving the cab. He would look for them, just as they were looking for him.

Imrich had two usual contact sites for Gabriel, one on the north side of the city, the other on the south side in a small street market. Gabriel would know that Bolan and Imrich would be heading south toward the compound, so it seemed a safe bet that he'd head in that direction, too.

Keeping a close watch on every detail in the dark streets around him, Bolan saw nothing that would lead him to believe he was being followed. More than likely, Smith and his men were tearing apart that small apartment and searching the bus station. With luck, in short order, he would get to confront Smith and take him out.

IMRICH REACHED THEIR rendezvous point first. Again he was glad to see her there and alive.

"The market," he said as she fell in beside him on the dark sidewalk. Around them families were going about their normal evening routines, and some of the children were starting to emerge to play outside as the heat of the day slowly lessened. The only light in the rough streets was from the open windows.

"I agree," Imrich said.

"Let's just hope Gabriel is thinking along the same lines," he said.

"Yeah," she replied. "If not, we're going to have to contact home one more time to figure out what they've found from the satellite feeds of the area."

"I really don't want to do that."

"Then let's hope Gabriel got out of that hotel and is waiting for us at this market."

"Alone," he said.

"Yeah, that would be nice," Imrich agreed.

THE MARKET WAS WELL LIT and teeming with shoppers. At least a hundred different booths and vendors lined the street, selling everything from fresh fruit to blankets and furniture. This wasn't an area of the city that tourists visited regularly, so the market catered to locals and their needs. There were no trinkets or funny hats to waste money on here. Clearly, the relative coolness of the evening compared to the heat of the day had brought the people out in droves, and in places the market street was shoulder to shoulder. The noise of hundreds of people talking and laughing seemed to echo through the two- and three-storied buildings that lined the nearby streets, and the smells of cooking food from the market mixed into a mouthwatering blend of richness and spice.

Bolan didn't much like the idea of leaving the dark side streets and walking into the bright light of the market, but it didn't appear they had much choice. They had circled the market once already and hadn't seen Gabriel's beat-up old cab.

The place that Imrich usually met Gabriel was near a booth of rugs and blankets near the center of the market.

"We can't go in together," Bolan said.

"Agreed. I blend in better than you do, so I'll circle around and I'll meet you on the other side."

He quickly handed her his pack. She was dressed like a local, so most wouldn't notice her. Unless they knew what or who to look for, of course.

"It wouldn't surprise me if Rija has some cameras in this area to watch Gabriel," she said. "I would, if I were him. So no matter what happens, we're going to have to move fast and get out of this area, just in case he happens to be monitoring."

"Right," Bolan said. "Meet you, and with luck, Gabriel, at that fruit stand we passed on the corner on the other side of the market."

He nodded and stepped toward the bright light of the market, checking to make sure that both of his guns were in position and within easy reach. Part of him felt as if he was walking into a trap, but at the moment, this was their only hope for getting to Rija's compound directly and, with luck, quickly enough to save the secretary.

He moved through the crowd, staying to the center of the street and being careful to not bump into anyone. He acted as if he had a destination, keeping his gaze forward and up, yet his head slightly down. He was far enough from the booths that no one tried to call him over or sell him anything. In fact, as far as he could tell, no one seemed to notice him at all.

He reached the area of the rug booth fairly quickly.

Thankfully, Gabriel was standing to one side, eating a tortilla, leaning against a building wall. He saw him and only nodded as he walked by, heading for the other side of the market. He didn't allow himself to even look back. Clearly Gabriel was also worried about the area being under surveillance, or he would have come out to greet him.

He made it to the other side of the market and crossed the intersection, moving into a darker side street where the night and lack of lights would hide him, and he could watch the market and not be seen.

Gabriel came out of the crowd about forty-five seconds later, moving slowly and finishing off his food. He ambled across the intersection toward Bolan, even though he was sure Gabriel couldn't see him in the shadows. As he got into the darkness of the buildings away from the bright lights of the market, he stepped forward.

"Good to see you again," he said.

"You too, Gabriel," Bolan replied, as they turned and kept walking away from the market. "Where's your cab?"

"Back near the bus terminal," he said. "I was caught up in the Smith roadblock and search, and decided to just park it and walk the rest of the way."

"We caused that, I'm afraid. Sorry."

"If we survive this," Gabriel said, shrugging, "it will still be there. And no worries, I know where there is a jeep we can use."

Bolan felt a slight bit of relief. The chances of survival and stopping Rija were much better with the three of them working together.

Less than a block later they joined up with Imrich.

"The arms dealer Cooper suggests is six blocks south of here," Imrich said to Gabriel after they shook hands in greeting.

"And the jeep we need is in a warehouse south of that,"

Gabriel said. "It seems for the moment that we are at least going in the correct direction."

"Sometimes you just get lucky," Imrich said with a smile.

They spread out along a two-block distance to make it less obvious they were walking together down the dark streets, then met up again at the address Brognola had given them for the arms dealer. It was a large house, maybe four stories tall, towering over the two-story houses tucked against it on both sides. The street was so narrow that the cars parked along both sides were mostly up on the sidewalks to leave enough room for a car to go down the street in one direction.

Imrich led them toward the building as Bolan kept one hand on his gun, watching for any movement from the shadows. There'd already been too many surprises on this mission, and he'd prefer to not have more.

Imrich pushed a button by the door and a moment later a rough male voice came from a speaker. "Yes?"

The man sounded English. Bolan turned sideways slightly so that he had his back to the wall and could see the street in both directions. Except for some family conversations, a number of kids playing a block over, and a loud radio, the night was quiet. No sound of any cars headed their way down the narrow street.

"A traveler from Wonderland to see you," Bolan said, giving the first part of the password sequence.

"May I ask the nature of your business?" the unseen man asked. Bolan placed his accent more firmly. Sounded like Manchester, and street poor, not upper-class.

"Two eggs and a grand slam breakfast," Bolan said, finishing the silly password sequence that played off a chain-restaurant menu.

15

Several door bolts clicked and released with an audible hiss, then the door slowly swung open. It was obviously much heavier than it appeared from the outside and the security more formidable.

As Imrich stepped into the darkness, Gabriel hesitated. "We need the weapons to stop Rija," she said. "For a lack of other choices, we've got to trust this guy."

Gabriel nodded, swallowed once, and then stepped inside. They followed quickly as the door hissed again and started to close.

The moment the door closed, the lights came up to show that they were standing in an entry area of beautiful tile, the floor covered partially with decorative rugs. The walls had ornate trim and were covered with numbers of large paintings in classic British art style.

A blast of air conditioning hit them, making Bolan's sweat chill in the wonderful, cool air. The night air outside had seemed chilly in comparison to the hot daytime temperatures. In here, it felt great. He had a hunch that this would be the last time he felt air conditioning for a while.

The Englishman came striding toward them in a brisk fashion. He was short, maybe five feet tall, and he wore a pristine black three-piece suit and tie with matching shoes. He even had a gold pocket-watch chain hanging out of one pocket and an unlit pipe in his hand. A faint odor of cognac-flavored tobacco seemed to come along with him.

"Friends of Hal Brognola's, I presume." He held up his hand before anyone said anything. "Please, no names. That wouldn't do for our business, not at all. Now follow me."

Imrich grinned at Bolan as the Englishman walked directly toward a wall and knocked a painting slightly sideways to the right. Then he reached over and slightly straightened another painting before repositioning the painting he had touched first.

It was likely that his fingerprints had been checked in that little activity, and that his eyes and face pattern had been scanned. Bolan had already noted the subtly placed cameras in the room, as well as the almost invisible gleam of electronic eyes in standby mode.

The wall slid aside without a sound, opening a large door onto a wide stone landing. A staircase led downward into pitch darkness.

"Do not start down the stairs without me," he said, indicating they should step onto the stone and wait.

Bolan once again had his hand on the butt of his Desert Eagle, just waiting for something to go wrong. The Englishman stepped onto the stone area behind them, moved to the staircase and tapped the top of the banister. The wall behind them slid closed just as silently as it had opened, and the staircase leading downward rose, converting into a staircase going up instead of down.

Now that was something Bolan had never seen before. He wondered what would have happened to someone who went down those stairs. Likely, from the Englishman's attitude and his security features, not anything pretty.

They followed him up the staircase and into a large room lined with beautiful oak cabinets, all closed. A marble-top table filled the center of the room. Someone seeing this room by accident would have thought it nothing more than a very, very large storage area.

"We're going to be in the jungle," Imrich said. "We need ammunition, weapons and explosives that we can carry at all times."

The Englishman just nodded.

As if by magic, every door and drawer in the room opened silently at the same time, exposing enough firepower to take down a small nation.

"Oh, my," Gabriel said. "I consider myself well-informed, but I have never imagined such a stockpile existed in 'Rivo."

Imrich just whistled softly.

Bolan felt just as surprised. He had been expecting a gun dealer in a back room, opening crates of weapons smuggled in from some black market dealer out of Russia or Israel. Not this. He stood near the table in the center and slowly turned and scanned the room.

Assault rifles of every make and kind, drawer after drawer of state-of-the-art pistols. There was a full wall of different kinds of explosives, and yet another wall of weapons, including a laser cannon that Bolan had only read about. He recognized most of the weapons and about two-thirds of the types of explosives. Where they were headed, he didn't want to trust their lives to anything experimental, so he planned on sticking with the tried and true.

He pulled out his two guns and held them up for the Englishman to see. "Ammo for these?"

He glanced at both and nodded, then moved to one wall, taking out two large boxes of magazines for each gun.

Imrich showed him both of her guns and the Englishman did the same for her.

Bolan took a moment to reload his pockets and put the rest in his bag as Imrich did the same with hers. There was no telling how much they were going to need, but he had a hunch that carrying as much as they could would be better, even with the extra weight.

"See something you like, Gabriel?" Imrich asked.

Gabriel nodded and pointed to an assault rifle and two different pistols.

The Englishman got both for him and a large number of rounds while Bolan studied the explosives. The walls of the compound that Rija had built looked too thick to be knocked down by anything they could carry. He still didn't have a plan for getting inside that compound. He would deal with that when they got there.

"What are the smallest and most powerful grenades you have?" he asked the Englishman.

The arms dealer moved to an open drawer on the explosives side, picked out a hand grenade the size of a golf ball and tossed it to Bolan.

The Executioner's stomach twisted as he caught the solid black explosive. It was as heavy as a baseball and he had no doubt he could throw it a pretty good distance if he had to. It had a small pin inserted into the center of the ball on one side.

"Delay time?"

"Six seconds," the Englishman said.

"Two dozen of these," Bolan stated, handing it to Imrich to look at.

He studied it for a moment, tossed it in the air once and caught it, making Gabriel's face go white in the process. "Make that three dozen. Each of us can carry a dozen."

"You might like these as well," the Englishman said.

He lifted two plate-size items from a drawer and handed one to him and one to Imrich.

Again there was a small pin that could be pulled to activate the explosive. They weighed just about as much as the balls.

"You throw them like a flying disk," Imrich said, pretending to toss the explosive.

"Correct," the arms dealer said. "They can be thrown up to 200 meters and have an explosive delay time of twelve seconds. They are very, very powerful and pack together without worry of explosion. Each of you could easily carry six of these, as well, into a jungle operation."

He glanced at Imrich and she nodded.

"Six each," she said. "And we need one sniper rifle."

"Two," Bolan added.

The Englishman pointed to one large area of a wall and indicated they should help themselves. Imrich picked out a rifle, and Bolan chose a brand new M110 SASS, the sniper rifle being phased into use by the U.S. Army to replace the M24, which had been the standard for the past twenty years. It had an attached suppressor, collapsible stock, and a Leupold scope. Semiautomatic rather than bolt action, it was a sniper weapon built for urban environments, but it would do just fine. Plus, Bolan liked the flexibility.

The image of the cleared area around the compound made the idea of a sniper rifle to take out some guards from the jungle edge a good idea. Both the rifle he picked and the one that Imrich chose had a sound-dampening feature on the barrel. It wasn't a silencer, since those cut accuracy, but it might confuse anyone looking for exactly where a shot came from in the distance.

And both could be broken down and put in a suitcase, which was critical since they still had to get out of the city alive.

He also added night-vision goggles for all of them and a heat-sensing scope.

His bag had suddenly gotten a lot heavier, with the rifle case and all the rounds and explosives. He made sure they were all riding easily and then put the bag over his shoulder, adjusting the strap.

Imrich did the same with her bag, and Gabriel struggled

for a moment with the large bag that the Englishman had provided for him.

Finally, they were ready.

"Make sure you charge our friend in Washington a lot for this stuff," Imrich said.

"You have no worry on that accord, madam," the Englishman said. "I will."

Imrich laughed as the Englishman led them out of the room and to the staircase.

"Go to the landing and wait," he said.

He shut the door at the top of the stairs and followed them down. As the arms dealer reached the landing, he touched two hidden buttons on the railing and the staircase lowered into the darkness again.

"At the bottom of the staircase you will find a door opening into a tunnel that will lead into more tunnels under the city. Where you exit the tunnels is none of my business. Once through the door, do not try to return. Is that understood?"

"Yes," Bolan said.

The Englishman nodded and handed them each a small flashlight, then he turned and vanished through a hidden door to the side of the stone landing area.

It was a brilliant way to protect his business. Clients entered through the front door and never left, at least that anyone could see.

Bolan led the way down the stairs, and as they reached the bottom, a faint light clicked on outside the open door. He went through, followed by Gabriel and then Imrich.

As they cleared the door, it hissed closed and then just vanished completely. Where it had been now appeared to be a century-old stone wall. Impressive, and one more reason the Englishman could keep his business going. That, and paying off a lot of officials, Bolan thought.

The tunnels smelled old and musty, and the dampness was more humidity than anything else.

"What are these tunnels?" Imrich asked.

Gabriel shrugged. "Remains of the old city, maybe. I've heard rumors of such things, but never seen them before. I always figured people were talking about the sewers and didn't know better."

"Let's just hope there are as many exits as the Englishman led us to believe," Bolan said. He turned and headed into the darkness, the small but powerful beam of the flashlight leading the way.

Gabriel turned on his light, as well, but Imrich said, "Keep that off and we'll stay close to Cooper. Who knows how long we're going to need these lights, or where they might come in handy."

Gabriel clicked off his light, and Bolan kept his light on the floor ahead of him to make sure of their footing.

After about fifty yards, they reached an intersection of the tunnels. Above they could hear some street traffic.

"I don't think we're that deep," Imrich said, looking up.

"And clearly we're not the first ones down here," Bolan said, shining his light on a few empty wine bottles and a worn mattress against one wall.

"So, which way?" Gabriel asked.

"You said you had a jeep," Bolan said.

"One from the airport," Gabriel said. "I know where it was left after the secretary's plane was attacked."

"And from the market, which direction and how far?" Bolan asked.

"South into the warehouse district," Gabriel said. "Twenty blocks, at least, from the market."

"So, we go as far as we can in that direction underground," Bolan said, pointing to the tunnel on the left. "That way."

"I do not like tunnels," Gabriel said as he started off.

"Neither do I," Imrich said.
"Safer than being on the streets," Bolan pointed out.
"If you say so," Gabriel said.
He didn't sound convinced.

16

The tunnels took them most of the way to the warehouse district, allowing them to come out in the basement of a small blanket shop that was closed for the night. They were careful to leave no sign that they had come through the shop, and Bolan doubted that even the store owner would know anyone had been in the place.

On the corner across from the store was a small restaurant that seemed about to close.

"We're going to need some food to make it through the rest of the night," Imrich pointed out.

"I agree," Gabriel said. "I am already very hungry."

Bolan had to admit that, even though he had been trying to ignore it, his stomach was protesting as well. And though they didn't have much time, he figured their only hope was to get something quick to last them.

The place had a dozen empty tables. Checkered tablecloths and large candles made it seem almost Italian, even though the menu was standard fare for 'Rivo.

When Imrich flashed a little extra money, the restaurant owner promised to be very quick and get their food at once after they had ordered.

"Look at this," Bolan said, taking a newspaper from near the front counter and laying it on the table in front of his companions. The headline asked the simple question. "Where is the American Secretary?"

"Time is growing really short," Imrich said after looking at the article.

"I don't know how much longer the President can keep a lid on this," Bolan agreed.

"I don't think we have much past dawn to get the secretary back," Imrich said.

Bolan glanced at his watch. "Seven hours to sunrise, but I doubt Rija will wait that long. If he knows we know where his compound is, he's going to move the secretary."

"So how long *do* we have?" Gabriel asked, looking very worried.

"If I know Rija, and I know him pretty well, we have about five hours, maybe less," Imrich said.

Bolan nodded.

At that moment their food came, and all three ate quickly in silence. At least they were going into the fight with a full stomach. They might not have more than a few hours to live, but at least if they died, they weren't going to die hungry. Still, Bolan didn't plan on dying—he planned on getting the Secretary of State out in one piece, and ending Rija's reign of terror, as well.

Twelve minutes later they were heading toward the warehouse district, but this time it was Gabriel leading the way, lugging his heavy bag. Bolan didn't much notice the bag on his shoulder. He had carried much heavier on many missions before.

What was laughingly referred to as the warehouse district was nothing more than a bunch of buildings, in different states of repair, jumbled together without any seeming order along the edge of the jungle. Some of the buildings looked as if they hadn't been used in decades and were about to collapse. Others looked fairly new in comparison, but clearly no one much cared about keeping anything up in this area. Some of the buildings were actually being claimed by the jungle on the south side.

"In here," Gabriel said softly, pointing to a side door of a building near the edge of the jungle.

"Left, right," Imrich whispered, drawing her guns as the two of them stood outside the door. "Gabriel, you stay out here and watch our backs."

Bolan couldn't see any indication of sensors or cameras watching the door or the area around the warehouse, but he had no doubt they were going to need to move fast. The three of them had been walking together through the warehouse district and more than likely some hidden camera had spotted them. Smith and his men could be headed there right now.

"Ready," he whispered, pulling both guns. He opened the door and went in to the right while Imrich went in left.

The pitch-dark warehouse echoed back the faint sounds of their movements. The floor was hard-packed dirt and the place smelled of mold and gunpowder, with the faint background odor of copper, meaning blood. It was also twenty degrees hotter inside than outside.

From the faint light coming from the outside, Bolan could see a light switch near the door.

"Lights coming up," he whispered to Imrich, then flipped the switch.

The faint lights overhead still seemed bright as the woman scanned the warehouse, ready to dive back out the door to cover.

But the warehouse was almost completely empty, with only a new-looking jeep tucked against the far wall.

Imrich went along one wall while Bolan searched the other, checking for any place that might give anyone cover. Not even an office inside this place. It was just four walls and a tin roof built over a dirt floor. A large number of bullet holes pockmarked the wood walls, and fresh casings from spent shells littered the floor. There were also some dark patches in the dirt that more than likely was blood. Clearly there had been a firefight in here recently.

"Clear," Imrich said to Gabriel as Bolan headed toward the jeep.

It was then that he noticed the foot hanging out of the jeep on the side near the wall. There was a body in the vehicle, more than likely an agent killed by Rija and left there.

He had just about reached the jeep when the body moved. Not threateningly, just slowly, as if waking up.

He moved up on the vehicle quickly. A man was sprawled across the two front seats, as if he had passed out there. As he pushed himself upright, Bolan recognized him from the briefing materials Hal Brognola had given him. Peter Cristoff, Secret Service agent. Presumed dead.

He sat up and then moaned, his hands holding his head, clearly not realizing Bolan and Imrich were there. Then he saw them and said, "Any chance you've got a couple of aspirin and a bandage for this head wound? I got a hell of a headache."

"Aren't you supposed to be dead?" Bolan asked, skipping the preamble.

"I suppose I am," he said. "Which means you know who I am, but I haven't a clue who you are."

"Matt Cooper," he said, holding out his hand, which the agent took, shaking it firmly. "This is Dusana and Gabriel. I'm glad to find you alive."

"It's good to be alive," he said. "Not that I deserve it."

Imrich fished into her bag for painkillers and a bandage for the bullet wound on his head. She handed over the pills along with a bottle of water, then got to work cleaning his head wound and bandaging it.

"Why don't you deserve to be alive?" she asked him as she worked. Her voice was soft and low.

"Because…I failed. The Secretary of State was kidnapped because I failed and…he's not dead, is he?"

Bolan shook his head. "Alive, as far as we know. We're en route to extract him."

"I would've expected…well, a different kind of team," Cristoff replied.

"It's complicated. Politics." That one word was enough to explain almost anything to those familiar with working for and in the government.

"How's your head?" Bolan asked, thinking of how painful his own wound had been.

He touched the bandage gingerly. "Better. Thank you."

Having another gun would help their chances, but it was a wonder that the agent was alive. No one else had survived. "So, what happened?" he asked.

"Rija and his men were waiting for us when we landed," he said. "They took the plane in less than two minutes."

Bolan shook his head. Something about the story didn't feel right. "I would've thought that the schedule for such an important visitor would be more secure than that. How did he know the details?"

Cristoff sighed softly and nodded. "It should have been. I…I gave Rija the information."

"You what?" Bolan said in disbelief.

He held up his hands. "I arranged to be on the protection detail—to lead it—and made a deal with another agent to help me. I made him think I was going to go through with it. But the whole time, I planned to betray them both. I wanted to be…" He stopped, gathered himself, then said, "There's no glory in it. We're invisible. And the best jobs, like guarding the President, are impossible to get. I thought if I…"

"Saved the secretary, you'd get your pick of assignments

and be a hero," Bolan finished. "How's that working out for you?"

"Easy, Cooper," Imrich said. "He did something terrible, but that doesn't make him a terrible person. What he did is understandable, especially if you think about what it must be like to stand in someone else's shadow every day."

"Anyway, the other agent—Diego Gonzales—must have contacted Rija. They expected me to double-cross them. Maybe he never believed me. He shot me and left me for dead. Somehow, I made it here, but I've been hiding ever since it happened and trying to figure out what to do. I don't know how to find Rija or…well, do much of anything. I just want to make things right."

"That's a tall order," Bolan said. "Where have you been hiding all this time?"

"I crawled into the jungle from the airport and worked my way around the edges of the city to here. When I arrived, there were some men emptying out this warehouse, so I waited until they'd left. I came inside and crawled into the jeep. That's about it. If you have any food, I'd be thankful."

Gabriel came up with some jerked beef strips and handed him one. "You are lucky to be alive," he said solemnly. "You could not make things right if you were dead."

"I want to, and I can help with one thing right away. The Secretary of the Interior is involved in all this—somehow."

"How do you know that?" Bolan asked.

"Because he planned the secretary's trip, arranged his schedule, all of it. When I first talked to Rija, he already knew those details and just wanted to use me to handle the security team."

Bolan nodded, thinking of Smith and the problems that he'd caused. He also had no further doubts about Imrich. Rija was a master manipulator, and like Cristoff, she had been used from day one to achieve his ends.

He forced himself to take a deep breath and put thoughts of seeing justice done for Rija out of his mind. Right now they had to get to Rija's other compound and get the secretary. And that was a long sixty-five miles of jungle from here.

"We need to get moving," he said. "I'm sure Smith and his men are on the way. And we're going to need transportation."

"What about this jeep?" Cristoff asked, looking puzzled.

Both Imrich and Bolan shook their heads at the same time.

"It was left here for a reason," the woman said. "Bugged, rigged to explode, there's no telling. Chances are there's a tracking device, at least, on it. With Smith in play and his access to the same resources as us, there are too many potential crossovers."

"I agree," Bolan said. He turned to Cristoff. "You up for joining us?"

"What's the mission?" he asked, his eyes clearing. "I personally have a United States Secretary to rescue and a traitor called Rija to kill." He paused, then added, "before I turn myself in to the authorities."

"That's the mission," Bolan said.

"Everyone needs to be clear about one thing," Imrich said, almost spitting out the words. "Rija is mine." She turned on her heel and headed for a side door out of the warehouse.

Behind her, Bolan quickly split some of his extra equipment with Cristoff, including a few of the explosives that he and Gabriel had been carrying.

As the soldier moved across the warehouse, he dug out the night-vision goggles and put them over his head so they would be around his neck. When he reached the door, he waited for Imrich to finish checking the door and made sure Cristoff was solid on his feet. Then, with Gabriel and Cristoff headed toward him, he reached to turn off the warehouse lights.

As the lights clicked off, Bolan ducked low and opened the door slowly, half expecting gunfire to cut through the wood.

Nothing. Yet.

The area outside the side door was pitch dark between the two buildings. He pulled the night-vision goggles down into place and eased outside. Everything was clear, with a slight green tint. He studied the area between the buildings in both directions. No one waited out there, so for the moment they were still ahead of Smith.

"Clear," he said, moving to the wall of a second building and taking up a covering position as the other three came out, making sure he kept a very close eye on Cristoff.

He was never going to turn his back on the agent, and from the way she was moving and staying behind Cristoff, Imrich wasn't either.

He had always just thought of any Secret Service agent as someone on the same side he was. Suddenly, with Smith being a rogue operative, and Rija having friends inside the U.S. government, he didn't dare trust anyone. At least not until all the players in this game were dead.

They headed back through the old buildings toward the front line of the warehouse district, with him leading, followed by Gabriel, Cristoff, and then Imrich. He stayed to the left and had Cristoff stay to the right so he could keep an eye on him while also watching ahead.

He was convinced that government troops or the Secret Police would be arriving shortly. They had sixty-five miles of jungle road to cover to get to the compound, and he remembered that road had a lot of twists and turns and hills to climb. The last thing they needed now was to alert Smith to their position or Rija to their arrival. There were just too many traps along the way.

They had to get out of this warehouse district as quietly as they could.

They had almost made it back to the cramped, narrow streets of the main part of town, when Imrich whispered,

"We have company coming in from the right flank, clearly headed toward the warehouse we just left."

Bolan glanced back at where the woman was staring at the heat sensor in her hand.

"How many?"

"Twelve," she said. "Piling out of two trucks two buildings over and heading toward us at a pretty good clip."

"Hide or take them out?" he asked.

"It will slow the enemy if we take these guys out," Imrich said. "And a dozen less troops we might have to deal with later."

"I agree," Bolan said.

"Yeah," Cristoff said.

"Gabriel, behind that wood." The Executioner pointed to a pile of lumber on the right. He didn't need to tell the other two agents what to do; they were already moving into perfect cross-fire positions.

"Gabriel," Bolan whispered, taking his position. "Don't fire until we do. Understand?"

"Yes."

He sounded very nervous, and Bolan didn't blame him. Better to test him here and now rather than depend on him later, when the odds would be even worse.

The soldiers clearly expected them to still be inside the warehouse, so they were not moving in any kind of defensive way, but simply half running in a group down the center of the road between the buildings.

It was going to be far easier than shooting fish in a barrel. These men would never know what hit them.

As the last man in the group passed them, the trio opened fire at exactly the same instant, followed a moment later by Gabriel.

He had been right. The soldiers didn't even get off a shot.

It was an ambush, not a fight.

As Imrich checked the heat sensor to see if there was anyone they had missed, Bolan went to check the pile of bodies now filling the road. As he figured, none of them were Smith. The agent would never be so stupid as to move into an enemy situation. But the new arrivals were wearing the same uniforms as the men who'd been with him earlier— Secret Police, then.

"No one else," Imrich said. "It's clear Gabriel."

He came out looking a little shaken. Then he went over to the pile of bodies and took a jacket and a hat from one of the men.

Bolan nodded. He was thinking clearly. He wouldn't doubt him again.

"To their trucks," Bolan said. "Looks like we found our ride."

"And our driver," Imrich said, as Gabriel put on the dead man's cap and slipped into his jacket, grimacing at the spatters of blood, but doing it all the same. "You're doing pretty good for a cab driver."

17

Imrich tapped lightly on the back window of the truck cab and mouthed, "Ten miles." Bolan nodded his understanding, relieved that they were getting close. The first fifty-five miles of the drive toward Rija's compound had gone quickly and without incident. Only six more miles remained before they'd stop, get out and go the last four miles on foot. Time was short, but approaching too close on the road, even in a government truck, wasn't a good idea. Just too easy for all of them to be killed at once.

Especially when Rija was expecting them at this point—he had to be—and Smith would be hot on their heels with the Secret Police. Smith had to know Bolan was still alive, and more than likely he already knew that there were four of them. Rija would have traps ready for them, but Imrich knew how he thought, how he believed he was better than any government agent. And that arrogant belief would be his downfall.

Gabriel had been driving, and since he knew the road pretty well, he had made great time, often sliding the truck sideways into a corner in the dark, only to expertly straighten it out on the other side of the corner without much loss of speed. Imrich was in the front seat with him, standing guard and checking the long-range heat sensor for any signs of trouble ahead.

Bolan and Cristoff were in the back of the canvas-covered truck on the benches used for hauling soldiers. Cristoff sat on one side, braced against the inside corner of the bed of the truck. He looked pale, and through a couple of the rough corners and sudden bumps, Bolan thought he might be sick, or pass out. Somehow the man managed to hang on, but Bolan wasn't certain how much good he was going to be to them without a rest. And they just didn't have time to rest at this point.

He checked his watch. Six hours until dawn.

Six hours was all the time they had to break into that compound and stop Rija before the island of Madagascar became an official war zone.

The ride in the back of the truck wasn't doing Bolan's head any good either, but he ignored it, as Cristoff was clearly trying to do. Bolan kept himself braced in the other back corner, facing Cristoff, one hand always on his gun. The exhaust of the truck sometimes got in under the back canvas flap and combined with the heat to make the bumping, swerving truck the worst ride of any carnival. A few times he regretted having eaten.

The loud engine noise made conversation impossible, even though Bolan desperately wanted to talk with the man to try to pin him down a little more on what had gone wrong. He didn't like not trusting him, but he just didn't have any choice at this point.

They were seven miles from the compound when Gabriel suddenly slowed.

"Hold on!" Imrich mouthed through the window.

"Hold on!" Bolan shouted to Cristoff.

Gabriel veered hard to the right and off the road, bumping up and down through a ditch and plowing into the brush of the jungle, making his own road where none had been before. The sound of vines snapping past and low-hanging tree branches brushing the vehicle echoed in the back of the truck.

Bolan managed to keep himself braced, but Cristoff didn't and went flying, tumbling hard to the floor between the benches. Just as suddenly, Gabriel slammed on the brakes and the truck stopped hard, banging the battered agent around even more.

Gabriel turned off the truck lights and the engine, and suddenly the loud, constant noise was replaced by dead silence. Bolan hoped like hell there was a good reason for the sudden detour into the foliage.

He slipped on his night-vision goggles and stepped over Cristoff, who looked dazed, then ducked out the back of the truck and dropped to the soft floor of the jungle. He didn't have time to take care of Cristoff at the moment. He needed to find out what was going on.

In front of him was the road and the trail left where they had plowed through the ditch and into the jungle. Anyone looking closely would see the tracks without a problem, but the truck was far enough into the brush to be hidden.

Gabriel came around from the driver's side of the truck, Imrich from the passenger's side. Both had guns drawn.

"We have company up ahead," the woman said, showing Bolan the heat scanner. "The signatures are blurry at this distance, but it looks like about fifteen to twenty men set up in positions on both sides of the road. I also took a reading behind us. There's another vehicle coming."

"Perfect," Bolan replied. "Well, it couldn't last forever."

"What?" she asked.

"Our luck. This is the Murphy's Law mission, remember?"

At that moment a low moan came from inside the truck and Cristoff stumbled out, holding his head and trying to get his night-vision goggles back in place.

"Are you all right?" Imrich asked, sounding concerned. "This isn't the—"

"I've been better," he snapped, straightening his back. "But I can fight."

"How far are we from the compound?" Bolan asked, knowing that dwelling on Cristoff's condition would be pointless.

"By the road, about seven miles," Gabriel said. "The road goes up and over a shallow ridgeline and then turns to the right on the other side. About four miles as the crow flies."

The rumbling of a truck started to fill the air and down the road the faint glow of headlights were starting to become visible.

"There's enough moonlight," Bolan said. "Take off the goggles."

As everyone removed them, Imrich asked, "So, do we fight those in front of us, those behind, or cut overland and hope to avoid both?"

Bolan grinned. "I think we're done running for now. We'll take out the truck coming up behind us, then we'll move right into that trap ahead. Let's reduce the odds while we can, and force Rija to burn more of his troops."

Imrich chuckled. "Between us, we can surely manage to get a grenade inside that truck."

"Cristoff, you're with me," Bolan said, wanting to keep him close enough to watch, in case he decided to switch teams, yet again. They moved quickly up the road, staying on the same side, while Imrich and Gabriel covered the place where they'd torn into the jungle with the truck. When they'd gotten a good twenty or so yards down the road, he turned to the agent.

"You stay here," he said. "I'll move farther down. Be ready."

Cristoff nodded and removed two grenades from his pack. "Copy that" was his only reply, his eyes focused on the road.

He moved deeper into the ditch, lying down, then taking his gun out and placing it within easy reach on the ground.

Bolan ran a good fifty paces down the road before ducking into the jungle. The heat was stifling, but he'd endured worse. The rumbling of the truck was getting louder by the moment. It was clearly a troop truck like the one they had taken.

Then, suddenly, the driver downshifted and Bolan could hear a second truck following it. He spun and noted that Imrich was watching him from a hidden position beneath the overgrowth. He held up two fingers, then three.

She nodded in understanding.

He grabbed three of the small golf-ball-size grenades out of his pack and held them ready. As the first truck cleared the corner two hundred yards back down the road, it was clear that they were facing three trucks, all full of troops headed to the compound. In total, there would be about forty soldiers.

Against just the four of them.

Under normal circumstances, he wouldn't be overly worried about the odds, but these were far from normal circumstances. This had been a mission of madness, with one thing going wrong after another. They had to take care of these soldiers and do it quickly. They didn't have time for a drawn-out firefight. As it was, the noise would likely bring the men from down the road—at least some of them—to investigate.

And they couldn't afford to lose anyone at this point.

The second truck cleared the corner not more than three truck lengths behind the first, catching all of the dust kicked up by the first vehicle. It was amazing the second driver could even see under those conditions.

The third truck followed at a more reasonable distance from the first two, and that would be the truck that Bolan would have to deal with, leaving the first two for the others.

He wished he had gone farther down the road, but now he didn't dare move.

He put two of the three grenades in his pants pocket and pulled both guns, one for each hand. He was going to have to trust that the other three would take care of the first two trucks. He had to get the third one.

The first truck sped past, the ground rumbling.

A moment later, the second went past, filling the air with thick, billowing dust from the rough road through the jungle.

He stood and stepped up to the edge of the road, facing the third truck as it sped toward him in the thick hanging dust. Over the low beams from the headlights he could see the driver's face, a confused expression showing that the sight of an armed man stepping out of the jungle surprised him. That fraction of a second brought him into range, and Bolan opened up with both weapons, blowing the windshield out and killing the driver and front passenger immediately.

The truck veered hard to the right, then slid left and tipped over onto its side. By the time it hit the road and began skidding down the rutted track, the Executioner had his pistol tucked away and a grenade in his hand. He quickly pulled the pin and rolled the grenade into the path of the sliding truck, then tossed a second one into the now open back of the vehicle. Some of the men in the back were injured already, moaning and screaming, but the terrifying shriek of one of them let Bolan know that he'd seen the grenade land.

Up the road, three quick explosions lit up the jungle, sending night birds shrieking into the air, as Bolan dropped back into the grass beside the road. A moment later the explosion on the track in front of him sent truck parts, debris, and human body parts flying in all directions.

He covered his head and waited as the disintegrating and burning truck slid past him, its forward momentum carrying it up and off the other side of the road. Anyone who survived both the crash and the explosions wouldn't be in any shape to get back in the fight. Still, it was best to be certain.

The Executioner stood and quickly put two shots into soldiers who were crumpled on the road but still moving, having been thrown clear in the initial crash. He had to eliminate all threats from behind. Then he turned and headed to the other side of the road to check out the wreckage of the truck itself. It was burning intensely, and there wasn't much left of it. No one was coming out of that truck.

Up the road, the other two trucks were also burning, and Imrich and Cristoff were also taking care of any still-moving soldiers. Besides eliminating a potential threat, it was more merciful than leaving them to the jungle predators that would find them as soon as the human interlopers moved away from the scene.

Somehow, he hoped that Smith was in one of those trucks, burning like a marshmallow over an open campfire, but he had a hunch that they weren't lucky enough to have killed the bastard that way. He was too smooth and had managed to stay out of the real fight every single time, using proxies to do his dirty work. Sooner or later, though, a reckoning would come, and Smith would be called to pay his tab.

When that time came, Bolan didn't think Smith would be able to afford the charges.

18

"Well, that was…loud," Imrich said with a tight grin when Bolan and Cristoff joined her and Gabriel on the road next to the burning trucks. "Do you suppose they heard all that up at the roadblock?"

"I think they heard that in the compound," Bolan said. "But we've got to get moving. They'll be coming along in short order."

"I agree," Cristoff said. "We're going to be like fish swimming upstream if we stay anywhere near this road. Rija will just keep tossing more and more soldiers at us. We don't want to get pinned down here."

"So we go cross-country, yes?" Gabriel asked. "I can't get the truck out of that jungle."

Bolan didn't much like the idea of heading out through the jungle, at least not at this point in the game. Aside from any man-made dangers that might exist, Mother Nature provided plenty of ways to get injured or killed—sinkholes, deadfalls and poisonous snakes, to name but a few.

He shook his head. "It would be too easy to figure out where we went in," he said. "Then we'd be traipsing around out there in the dark with Rija's men behind us."

"And this means?"

Bolan peered down the road. "I'd rather go through those men up ahead of us, and get to that ridgeline you mentioned.

We can leave the road there and keep our backs clear of trouble."

"It will be easier to hide our trail and defend ourselves from there than it will be wading through the jungle," Imrich agreed.

"So we need to get through the men ahead of us," Cristoff said.

"And we're going to have to get clear of these fires before the heat sensor's going to work again," Imrich reminded them. "How do you want to do this?"

"We'll cut into the jungle a ways from the truck, leaving a trail to make them think we went in there," Bolan said. "There's no telling for sure who's behind us, but we know Smith is around somewhere. Then we'll get back on the road and take out the soldiers up ahead. If they're spread out enough, we might be able to take out a good number of them without shooting, go back to the truck and make them think we followed the road up to the soldiers. The way they're spread out, we might be able to take a number of them without firing a shot."

"Sounds like a plan to me," Imrich said. "Time is wasting, and we still have a mission to finish."

As they headed back to the truck, the smell of burning human flesh started to fill the air around them. In spite of everything Bolan had ever experienced, it was a smell he never got used to, and he'd be glad to be away from the area.

When they reached the truck, everyone grabbed their packs and water bottles then headed into the jungle with their night-vision goggles firmly in place. The evening was still hot, humid, the air almost thick enough to see. The lingering smoke from the burning trucks didn't help matters, but Bolan thought they'd go out quickly. It was too damp for anything to burn for very long in this place without constant tending or additional fuel.

Imrich was on point, followed by Gabriel, then Cristoff, with Bolan last, about twenty steps behind Cristoff. Before leaving the truck, Imrich warned the Secret Service agent of the kinds of traps that Rija liked to set in jungles. "I know his style," Imrich said. "He's predictable and hasn't ever planned a trap I haven't been able to spot."

"That's probably why you're still alive," Cristoff said. "And why he valued you."

"Let's go see if we can change his mind about that," she replied.

It was obvious to Bolan that Cristoff was warming to Imrich quickly. It was easy enough to do. She was upbeat, often dryly humorous, and a capable killing machine. Of course, that described Rija, as well. Except Imrich was loyal to the people and their cause, and Rija was a traitor.

A soon to be very dead traitor.

One hundred yards from the guards, Imrich stopped, and they gathered around the heat sensor that showed exactly where each guard was to plan their attack. It turned out that there were only twelve men in total, six at the roadblock and six others in cross-fire positions in the nearby jungle. The six on the road would be easy to take once they got the others in the jungle.

Bolan glanced at his watch, then he turned to the cab driver who was clearly not happy to be in the jungle. "Gabriel, find a position so that you have an open shot at those guards in the road. Just don't get seen and don't shoot until you hear us firing."

The cab driver nodded and then swallowed hard.

"We take the three on this side of the road at the same time," Bolan said. "Silently, if possible. I'll take the one on the south, Dusana center, Cristoff north. If we can't take them silently, we eliminate the guards on the road, blow up their truck and ignore the guards on the other side. Keep moving up the road to the ridgeline."

Imrich agreed, then patted Gabriel on the shoulder. "I'll come back for you if that happens."

"Thank you," Gabriel said, looking slightly relieved.

"Seven minutes," Bolan said, glancing at his watch.

The other two did the same, and as the second hand hit the top, he said, "Mark."

As a unit, the three of them turned and headed into the jungle. Once Imrich and Cristoff were out of his sight, he couldn't hear either of them.

With twenty seconds to spare, the Executioner reached the first guard's position. The guard wasn't wearing night-vision goggles and was staring intently down the road toward the burning trucks, looking very worried.

Bolan moved in behind him and, right on the mark, slit his throat while yanking the gun from his hands so he couldn't get off a warning shot. He eased the body quietly to the soft jungle floor and waited for Cristoff and Imrich to join him. They hadn't made a sound.

Once they were back together, they coordinated their attack on the remaining guards and crossed the track in the dark on the other side of the roadblock. Again, they took out all three targets without a sound.

Clearly these were Rija's men, not Smith's. Maybe they should have just allowed the trucks through and let the two factions fight it out, Bolan thought.

The only thing that bothered him was why Rija would put a guard post here, where it would be almost impossible to defend against any kind of attack from just about any direction. Clearly, he had been using these men as a warning signal.

With six quick shots, the three of them took out the guards on the road without the guards even firing a round.

"How about we use that truck to save a little time?" Cristoff suggested, pointing to the guards' truck as the three of them climbed up on to the road.

"No," Imrich and Bolan said at the same time.

He had no doubt at all that Rija would use that truck as a trap, expecting them to do exactly what they had just done. These men weren't highly trained soldiers. More than likely they were new recruits who had drawn the short straw.

"Probably rigged to be traced," Imrich said. "In spite of his predictability, Rija learned a lot from me and he's trained for years. He knows every trick and will use them to kill us."

Bolan didn't say anything. Imrich was right. And from here on, they were on Rija's ground. Bolan had no doubt that Rija would control them as much as he could.

Imrich waved for Gabriel to join them.

With every passing second, Bolan was getting more and more worried. So far, this had been too easy. And nothing about Rija was easy unless he wanted it to be. Chances were that Rija was watching them right now, more than likely just laughing. He would love this sort of cat and mouse game, and he was one of the best at it. But this time, the mouse was going to bring down the cat.

They started off again with Imrich on point, moving up the left tire track of the road. Bolan let himself look around. They were climbing a slight ridgeline, similar to one he remembered from his trip to the compound. On both sides of the road, the jungle was thick, with tall trees and underbrush that was easy to move through if a person went slowly enough.

The night air felt stifling from the heat of the day, and no wind blew at all. The jungle was scented with thick, dark dirt, odd flowery smells that reminded him of a perfume store, and the mold that came with the dampness and high humidity. It would have been a nice night to enjoy a walk if not for the fact that two armies wanted to kill them.

"There is an intersection over the hill just ahead," Gabriel whispered. "It comes in from the city as well, going through a small town about seven miles over."

"So we go cautiously," Bolan said, glancing at his watch. Every time they had to do this, they were losing time, valuable time that it would take to get into the compound and get the secretary.

At the crest of the hill, he stopped them and pointed to the right. "We go up the ridgeline."

Imrich glanced at Cristoff. "Ridgelines are something Rija trained every soldier to stay away from. Too dangerous and exposed from too many sides. He would not expect us to go that way."

As they climbed the slight incline, Bolan could still see the fires from the burning trucks lighting up the night sky and the jungle around them. They had traveled for almost ten minutes, making good time, when suddenly Cristoff brought them to a halt, pointing to the heat sensor in his hand. On the ridgeline ahead, more than a dozen men were heading slowly toward them, spread out in a military formation. These were trained soldiers, rather than cannon fodder. Bolan had no doubt about that.

"We go down toward the road and into the compound," Bolan said. They were still three miles out and there was a lot of jungle between their position, and Rija and the secretary. Getting into a firefight every time they ran into a group of soldiers wouldn't allow them to cross the distance in time.

The intersection was now behind them. One road from 'Rivo was blocked by the trucks, but the other road was still open.

Below them, the road from the intersection to the compound ran between two small hills through a shallow valley that wasn't more than a half mile long if he remembered right. The heat sensor showed the formation of men behind them on the ridge passing and heading down the ridge toward the flaming trucks. So much for Rija not using the ridgeline to move men. He had clearly thrown out the playbook and improvised, trying any tactic to win, no matter how many men he lost in the process. And, since many of them were pressed into service, using them as cannon fodder didn't bother him. He would simply hit the next town and find some more.

As they reached the road, the heat sensor showed the surrounding area clear.

Then, suddenly, having hidden from their heat sensor on the other side of the shallow hills, at least two dozen men rose and started down toward them at an almost full run. Clearly some of them had night-vision goggles from the speed they were moving through the brush.

Smith's men, Bolan was sure of that. They weren't moving in any type of military formation as Rija's men would do.

"Take cover!" Cristoff shouted.

Cristoff, Imrich and Bolan spread out and took up positions in the ditch about the same distance apart. Gabriel ended up beside Cristoff.

The point men appeared on the other side of the road and Bolan took down the two on his side, while Imrich took out two in the middle, and Cristoff and Gabriel dropped another two on their side.

The men behind the attackers all dived for cover and returned fire.

The sound of the gunfire echoed through the jungle around them, and Bolan had no doubt that if they didn't make quick work of these men, the men from the ridge would come down behind them. And the last thing he wanted was to be trapped between Smith's men and Rija's men, stuck in a ditch with no cover and no decent way out.

He grabbed one of the explosive disks from his bag and held it out, shouting for Imrich to glance his way.

She did and nodded and dug into her pack, shouting to Cristoff to dig one out as well.

When Cristoff was ready, Imrich counted them down, lowering her fingers one at a time, and they all pulled the pins and threw the bombs at once while Gabriel gave covering fire.

The black disk disappeared from Bolan's hand into the dark night. Even the night-vision goggles couldn't follow the thin black disk, which meant no one on the other side would see them coming either.

The fight went on, the seconds passing slowly as they exchanged fire. Bolan could feel and hear the bullets whisking just inches above his head.

A couple of shots slammed into the ground in front of him, showering him with pebbles and dirt. At the exact count, he ducked his head and yanked off his night-vision goggles as Imrich did the same, to make sure they wouldn't be blinded by the flash of the blast.

The three combined explosions ripped a huge hole in the edge of the jungle across the road and injured two of Smith's men who were screaming in pain, running in circles as flames ate their clothes and skin.

Imrich killed both of them before Bolan could get his gun back up.

Staying in the ditch and keeping his head down so that he couldn't be seen from the other side of the road, he moved to Imrich's position and tapped her on the shoulder as he went by, indicating she should follow him. They needed to get away from the scene and keep moving toward the compound. Anyone who was still alive in that bunch would be headed back into the jungle.

As he reached Gabriel, the man started to stand, but Bolan held him down, indicating he should remain silent and stay crouched in the ditch in case of stray fire from the other side.

Cristoff was stretched out in a firing position on the ground on the nearby bank. Bolan went to nudge him and realized something was wrong.

He wasn't holding on to his gun. It had slipped into the grass beside his hand.

Bolan eased him over and Cristoff flopped onto his back, his arms spread wide. A round bullet hole dripped blood in the middle of his forehead.

"Crap," Imrich said from beside him.

Bolan felt his stomach sink a little. Three operatives had a lot better chance than two, considering what they were facing. The task ahead just got that much more impossible. Still, at least the man had died trying to do the right thing and make up for his horrible mistake.

He picked up the heat sensor from the grass beside Cristoff and checked it. It was still working, but the battery was getting low. Imrich transferred Cristoff's grenades and ammunition to her pack.

The sensor told him that Rija's men on the ridgeline were slowly heading toward the firefight's location. They were being cautious. He could see a number of bodies on the other side of the road, but none of them seemed to be moving at the moment. They would let Rija's men clean up the mess when they arrived. Right now, they needed to get to the compound.

He pulled the phone out of his pocket and ejected a small tracker, placing it on Cristoff's body. Bolan silently nodded his thanks to his fallen comrade and would make certain he made it home with the rest of them when it was all over.

He had been close to a number of agents over the years who'd lost their lives on missions. He knew, just as Imrich knew, that they would never be remembered beyond a few friends, their service often unacknowledged. Every agent knew that going in. Cristoff had done something horrible, but that didn't erase his prior service.

He turned his back on Cristoff's body and moved along the ditch toward the compound.

Behind him he heard Imrich push Gabriel out ahead of her with a gentle "Let's go."

Chances were that some or even all of them would end up joining Cristoff. It was a chance they all had to take. Death was one of the risks.

Dealing it out, however, was their job. And Bolan intended to do his very well.

19

Bolan estimated they were within two miles of the compound. They had been almost running down the road, moving as quickly in the dark night as they dared, circling off the road just once, to hide when a pair of trucks went past, going in the opposite direction. Most likely they were headed for the roadblock to see why someone hadn't checked in.

At one ridgeline, where the road cut over and down the other side, they moved off the road and up into the jungle again to make sure that no one was hiding on the far side, out of sight of their heat sensor.

"Another road...comes in from the left...a half mile ahead," Gabriel said, breathing like a winded horse and pointing into the darkness. He wasn't wearing night-vision goggles. "Now would be a good time to rest," he added, sinking down to sit on the jungle floor.

"Does the road come from 'Rivo?" Imrich asked.

"Not directly, but yes, it's possible someone could come from that way."

Bolan didn't like the sound of that at all. Walking this line between Smith's commandeered Secret Police and Rija's soldiers made the odds much worse. And he kept having the feeling that he was doing exactly what Rija wanted him to do. He hated that feeling, but couldn't shake it and didn't know what to do to avoid it.

Earlier, he'd been concerned that Rija might have cameras hidden along the road, but Imrich assured him that it was very unlikely. They'd tried it at the main compound and found that between the humidity, storms, and even interference from the many birds living in the jungle, it wasn't practical.

"Besides," she'd quipped, "if he had cameras, they wouldn't be looking for us. They'd have *found* us."

Bolan had to admit she was right, and to make it to the secretary in time, the road was really their only choice. Still, even Rija had to know their general location, so at some point very soon, they'd have to figure out a way to disappear into the jungle and get into the compound, surprising those inside at least a little bit. He had no idea how, just yet, but sometimes he didn't know how he was going to accomplish a mission until faced with the problems in the field.

The images of a dozen men on the ridgeline came into range of the heat sensor. They were moving through the jungle in a standard formation, spread out in a loose phalanx, with two-man teams. Rija's men.

"We have to get moving," Bolan said to Imrich and Gabriel, who were both using the momentary breather to drink from their water bottles. He gave her a glance at the heat sensor screen showing the approaching men, and she nodded.

"Looks like they are pushing us back toward the road again," she said.

"Getting that same feeling," he agreed, tucking the scanner into his pack. "But at the moment, we don't have much choice, do we?"

"None," Imrich said. "We're just puppets on a string. I'll take point."

Gabriel dropped in behind the woman as she started toward the compound, angling through the jungle to come out on the road after a few hundred paces.

Bolan came up last, listening for any sounds ahead or any

sign of a vehicle moving through the night on the road. They made good time over the next half mile and just before the intersection, he had them stop off to one side of the road. He again checked the heat sensor.

It lit up like the lights on a Christmas tree.

He and Imrich both dived for cover, yanking Gabriel down into the ditch beside them. The entire intersection ahead of them and both sides of the road leading to the compound were surrounded by almost fifty troops.

Now he understood what Rija had been doing. He had been having his men drive them directly into an ambush.

"Smith's men?" Imrich asked.

"No way of knowing," he whispered back.

"We're trapped," Gabriel said, his voice rising slightly after looking at the heat scanner.

"Not yet, we're not," Imrich said.

Rija's men were still not in range of the sensor, but Bolan had no doubt they were heading in this direction, pushing them right into the ambush.

From what he could tell, there was just no way around them without going a good mile or more out of the way, and Bolan's team didn't have the time for that. They were going to have to go right through the men ahead of them, one way or another.

The Executioner carefully studied the heat signatures of all the soldiers. Chances were most, if not all of them didn't have night-vision goggles, so they were sitting there waiting, trying to use the moonlight to see past the shadows of the vines and trees surrounding them.

"How far do you think you could throw one of those explosive disks?" he asked Imrich, pointing to a group of a dozen soldiers on the left of the sensor screen

She studied it for a moment. "Maybe that far."

"We toss two disks in that direction and then we move

right, working through the men guarding that side of the road."

Imrich nodded. "We toss the disks first and move, then, when we're close, we toss a few more grenades into the center of the intersection to cut off any help coming toward us as we try to get through. If we're going to stir up an anthill, we might as well really give it a good mix."

"Agreed," he said.

Bolan turned to Gabriel. "Stay between us and move as silently as you can. We'll get through this."

He nodded.

"Make sure you got a grenade in your pocket and extra magazines where you can get to them quickly," Imrich said as she patted Gabriel on the back.

Bolan dug out the disk-shaped explosive from his pack and hefted it, trying to get a sense of the angle to toss it to get the most distance. Overthrowing in this case would be better than underthrowing.

"Ready?" he asked.

Imrich had an explosive in her hands as well. He looked at the heat sensor, spotting the direction once again that they had to toss the disks, and then nodded. "Count of three."

"One, two, three," Bolan said, yanking out the pin. In complete unison with Imrich, he tossed the disk, using all his strength to throw it high and long.

The two black bombs vanished instantly into the darkness of the night sky.

Imrich, with two guns drawn, turned and headed up the ditch beside the road toward the compound and straight at the men standing guard.

Bolan pushed Gabriel to follow and fell in behind them, his guns also out and ready.

No sounds cut the night, and even Gabriel's steps in the jungle beside the road were almost silent. Clearly the cab driver had spent a little time in the jungle outside of the paved streets of 'Rivo, in spite of the fact that he wasn't in shape.

When the countdown was close, Imrich stopped and pulled off her night-vision goggles, ducking. Gabriel almost ran over her, but she yanked him to cover as well.

Bolan tore his own goggles off and crouched, quickly putting both guns away and grabbing two of the small round grenades in his right hand.

Imrich was reaching for hers when the two disks exploded, lighting up the jungle and shaking the ground under them. Shouts and screams filled the air, and a dozen wild shots were fired at the same time.

Bolan nodded to himself in satisfaction. Clearly one of their throws had been right on target.

Imrich gave him a thumbs-up and winked, then counted down on her fingers: Three. Two. One.

They each threw another grenade into the center of the men on the left of the intersection, then another closer to the middle of the intersection and one more just beyond it.

An instant later, Imrich was up and moving toward the guards on the right of the road, night-vision goggles back in place. Bolan and Gabriel jumped up right behind her, moving silently and quickly. The big American left his goggles off, trusting Imrich to lead the way.

Shouting and more shots echoed through the night as the frightened soldiers fired blindly into the jungle nowhere near where their three attackers ran. The smell of burning trees and grass wafted through the air, and the smoke was blowing slightly toward them, making Bolan's eyes sting a little.

As his count ended, Imrich ripped off her goggles and again ducked, lying flat on her stomach in the shallow ditch to the right of the road. He and Gabriel did the same, keeping a distance between each other. As far as Bolan could figure, they were very close to the right side of the line of solders.

The second round of explosions ripped through the soldiers on the other side of the road, and then the second grenades went off, very close to the intersection. The blast concussion again shook the ground.

Now the shouting and anger and shots increased as the soldiers fired into the jungle in all directions.

"Hold your fire!" a commanding voice echoed out over the jungle.

Bolan slipped on his night-vision goggles and tried to spot who was in charge.

The voice had come from slightly up the road, near the intersection behind the line of soldiers. Bolan could barely make out the shape of a jeep tucked off the road in the jungle.

One man climbed up onto the front of the vehicle and shouted, "Stay in position."

It was Smith. Bolan grabbed his night-vision binoculars to be sure.

"Smith," he whispered to Imrich.

The yelling and shouting and firing by the solders slowly started to decrease.

Smith again shouted for his men to remain in position and stop firing blindly into the jungle.

Imrich yanked open her pack and pulled out the long-range rifle. Within seconds she had it completely together and loaded and steadied on the bank. Bolan was impressed. He didn't know many people who could have put that gun together that fast.

Smith still stood on the jeep, shouting more instructions to his men. Now the firing had almost stopped.

"Toss two more grenades across the road," Imrich hissed.

Gabriel grabbed one and waited until Bolan indicated he should pull the pin. He tossed the bomb with a slight grunt. A second behind him, the Executioner tossed his grenade, staying low and out of the line of fire.

Once again he looked through the night-vision binoculars at the traitor. Smith wasn't just a rogue agent, he was working with others who would undermine the government. And his loyalty was only to money.

Imrich lined up her shot through the night scope, then stopped. "It's yours," she said, sliding the weapon over to him. He nodded and picked it up, repositioning it quickly and finding his enemy through the scope.

He placed the crosshairs carefully, breathed in once, then squeezed the trigger. The bullet took Smith in the side of the head, sending him cartwheeling backward off the seat of the jeep and onto the hood. His blood appeared as a dark, ugly blob on the windshield, and Bolan had no doubt that the shot had been a clean one.

In the darkness of the jungle, his shot sounded like just another wild shot from one of the soldiers, and no return fire came at them.

Mr. Smith, or whatever his real name was, was dead. It was as if a very heavy weight had suddenly been lifted from Bolan's shoulders, a weight he hadn't even realized he was carrying. Finally, the man had met his end. He'd leave Hal Brognola to uncover the rest, but Bolan's part was done.

Two other men in the jeep jumped out to check on their leader, who lay crumpled in the grass.

There would be nothing to check on with a rifle that powerful; a direct shot to the head didn't leave much behind. He stared at the scene so long, he barely got the night-vision glasses away from his eyes before the first of the two grenades exploded across the road, for an instant lighting up the jungle as if it were a bright, sunny day.

Imrich had the rifle put away and her pack on her back as the second grenade exploded and the wild shooting and men crying out again filled the night air. "Nice shot," she said. "I can't think of a man who deserved it more, except Rija. Let's go give him the same, shall we?"

"Absolutely," he said.

He moved up beside her and handed her the heat sensor. It showed five soldiers on the right side of the road that stood between them and the compound.

"I'll take these," he said, pointing to the three on the right. "You take those two. Gabriel, stick with Dusana. No need to stay silent."

Thirty seconds later they had killed the five soldiers, who were too panicked to put up much of a fight

Bolan and Imrich had done exactly what Rija wanted them to do: they had removed a link between himself and the U.S., while forcing the two operatives to exhaust themselves elsewhere.

He was being used and he hated that feeling.

20

They were still a good quarter mile from the compound when Imrich stopped them. The night air had finally started to cool off a bit, and there was no wind. They had about three-and-a-half hours until sunrise.

"Do you have any idea what this place is going to be like?"

"Based on the information that Gabriel has given us, and the historical data that Hal Brognola pulled for us on the fort, I have some idea. The dense jungle makes it difficult, but Hal was also able to capture some satellite images for us."

Bolan pulled out his phone and began to pull up the 3D version of what the satellite had gathered and the little bit of information that Gabriel had been able to glean from the locals.

"From what we can tell, this is a very traditional French fort. The walls are only three stories tall with a bastion at each corner."

"What is a…bastion?" Gabriel asked

Bolan punched a couple of keys and a diagram of a bastion appeared on screen.

"The bastion resembles the old medieval towers in a castle. The shape isn't round, but angled like the top of a pentagon. The design pushes the ledge out farther than the main wall, making it almost impossible to scale if the fort is under siege."

Gabriel nodded. The closer they got, the more worried he

was about breaching the walls of that compound in any direct manner. Rija had designed and retrofitted the place, using what he'd learned from Imrich, and Bolan had no doubt he'd made plans for just about any standard attack. So the key was to take a nonstandard run at it.

He quickly checked the heat sensor to see if any troops were close. None were at the moment, but it seemed likely that Rija knew they were getting close, even if he didn't know their exact location at the moment.

Bolan faced Imrich and Gabriel. "It's a large compound covering the size of about a standard city block, maybe more. The walls are a thick adobe meant to withstand cannon fire. They are about five yards thick, and guards in teams of two walk the tops of them. The satellite images have guards patrolling the walls and posted at each of the bastions."

"So much for blasting our way through the walls," Imrich said.

"Not a chance that way," Bolan told them. "Those walls might be able to hold off rocket launchers without much of a problem."

Gabriel said something softly that Bolan didn't catch, but he was sure it wasn't good. The man had become more and more silent as the fighting had grown. He'd done a great job helping them and not holding them back in any way, but this fight would be way out of the league of such a small group, and they all knew it. Whatever they planned, it had all the hallmarks of the impossible.

"There are floodlights spaced along the walls," Bolan said, going on, "that will light up the open area around the walls. The edge of the jungle is a good hundred running paces from the walls, and is more than likely mined."

"A kill zone," Imrich said.

"Exactly," Bolan replied. "But very nicely landscaped to look safe. There are electronic eyes along the tops of the walls that would detect anyone coming at them and activate a series of lasers to track and any intruder and make them easier to kill."

"So, no frontal assault," Imrich said. "Got that. How do Rija's troops get in and out?"

"A horn-activated system on the vehicles that is changed frequently, just like you had designed for the other compound."

"Frequency-modulated sound waves controlled by a remote computer in a security center," Imrich said, nodding. "If one of the trucks is captured, they simply change the frequency on all of them except the missing one. So, I'm a tech freak, what can I say? I like to keep up on what's out there and what he's got there is state-of-the-art. Sadly, I made sure of that. I gave him all the best knowledge I had, and now it's going to be used against us."

"Any chance we can use what you know to get in there?" Bolan asked. "Any bug in the system that you know about?"

Imrich shook her head. "Just getting a vehicle that has an up-to-date frequency and not having the guards do a visual on the drivers."

"Tough to do on the second part," he said. "All the vehicles I saw that they used were open-air jeeps. The guards are going to easily spot anyone who doesn't belong and kill them."

"So, what's inside the walls?" Imrich asked after a moment of silence.

"A courtyard runs around most of the inside of the walls, made to look decorative and very ornamental, like a mansion's grounds, but designed to be very difficult to cross. Again, a replica of the other compound, only the buildings are older. Even the fountains have been redesigned with hidden weapons that can be brought out by remote control from a security center."

"Another killing ground on the inside of the walls as well," Imrich said, nodding her appreciation at Rija's design.

"As you come in through the main gate, on the right there is a long, low building made out of the same fire-resistant adobe. It appears to be a large barrack that could hold upward of three hundred men, more if it has a second floor underground. Another long building runs parallel to the barrack, and behind it looks to be some kind of storage building. Both of them were designed for functionality, rather than style, but the main house is a different story altogether. He took all of the best pieces of the French ingenuity and enhanced them with modern technology."

"How's that?" Imrich asked.

"Looks like it's the main officers' quarters," Bolan said. "Two levels and designed like a French villa. In the front is a large set of stairs that leads up to the double doors. Windows look out on the courtyard and the jungle, but are covered by heavy bars."

"I would imagine the walls are thick as well," Imrich said. "And he'll have cameras everywhere, most hidden. If they have the same controls that we do at the other compound, the access is a palm scanner in the wall and the doors have internal bars. The doors open outward as well."

"Rija thought of every detail, didn't he?" Bolan asked.

"Every detail," Imrich replied.

"We are so screwed," Gabriel said.

Bolan had to agree. Now that they were this close, he still hadn't come up with an idea of how to get into that compound and rescue the secretary in the next few hours. Even trying seemed like sure death, and he wasn't that excited about giving his life for no reason. He didn't mind taking risks for his country, but a suicide mission without reaching their objective didn't make sense.

"How about we go back to town and call in an air strike?" Imrich said. "Let the Feds get someone to just drop a couple of bunker-buster bombs on the place."

Bolan knew that the woman was only half kidding. "I wish," he said. "But you and I both know the results of the Secretary of State getting killed down here. The entire region might go up like a forest fire on a hot summer day. Worse, if Rija pulls this off, every person we send overseas will be at risk for the same treatment."

"So we make a run at getting in there," Imrich said, sighing. "But how, without killing ourselves in the process?"

Bolan let the silence of the jungle slowly press in on them. No heat signatures of any of Rija's men had yet to show on the heat sensor, which seemed odd. He knew that Rija had to know they were coming close, and he wouldn't ignore someone pressing down on him, no matter how strong he thought his walls were.

"So, Rija's deadline is sunrise," Bolan said, looking at Imrich. "You think he'll wait until then before moving the secretary?"

"I do," Imrich said. "He still thinks that his demands will be met. He has to know we're here, so we're the only threat to him, and out here, we don't look like much of a threat. He has no reason to speed up his plans."

"I agree," Bolan said, knowing that she was completely right about Rija. His ego alone would keep him on time with this operation. "So back to the question of how we get in."

Imrich glanced at the heat sensor to see that it still showed clear, then said softly, "Did you say there were fountains in the courtyard with hidden weapons?"

Bolan nodded. "There are."

"Underground," Imrich said. "When we built the other place, I put all security and other defense features underground. Because it's an old structure, he would have to do the same because there is no internal support system for it."

"You're right," Bolan said. "A lot of that compound has to be underground. And Rija would never allow himself to be trapped inside that compound if it was surrounded and under attack. He would have more than one escape route."

"Any helicopter pad that you noticed inside the walls?" Imrich asked.

"None that I saw," he said. "And besides, escaping by air would be far too dangerous. He would vanish into the jungle."

"So the way in is his way out," Imrich said. "More than likely heavily protected and hidden, but we have a better chance going in through one of his escape hatches than going through that front gate."

"I agree completely," Bolan said. "But Rija is going to figure that's what we're doing."

"So we distract him a little," she replied. "How many of those explosive disks do we have left?"

Between them they had four.

"Here's what we do," Imrich said. "Gabriel and I will go to the right and circle around, looking for any kind of sign or formation or building that would make an emergency exit. You head up the road until you get close enough to toss a few of those disks at the walls. With luck, you might sail one over and inside. Then cut left into the jungle and look for anything on that side of the compound."

"Meet exactly in the center of the compound on the opposite side, about a hundred yards into the jungle," Bolan said, agreeing to the plan. It wouldn't fool Rija beyond a slight surprise, but it might stir up the guards a little.

"Let's do it," Imrich said.

Bolan checked the heat sensor to see if there were any soldiers of either army close by, then handed the sensor to Imrich and headed back toward the road, moving silently and watching for any traps along the way.

Near the right edge of the road and about a hundred yards from the clearing, he spotted a very well-hidden explosive trap set for anyone moving down the ditch. From that point forward, there were traps and trip wires in the ditch every ten steps or so.

He moved carefully, yet as fast as he could in the darkness until he was close enough to finally see the compound walls ahead. The lights were on, yet weren't as bright as he expected them to be, and the walls were a little closer to the jungle than he originally anticipated. From where he was, he would be able to easily sail a disk or two over them.

He got into a position near the edge of the cleared jungle and got ready to throw.

At that moment, a jeep horn blew on the inside of the gate and the guards on the walls looked down as the gates started to open.

Bolan tossed the first explosive disk over the wall of the compound. If he was lucky, it would land near one of the barracks.

One second later, the second disk was on its way, just as the gates came fully open and two jeeps, each carrying four men, drove out. Bolan couldn't follow the flight of the dark disks against the night sky, but no alarms sounded. It seemed that all the attention of the guards was on the two departing jeeps.

Bolan reached into his bag and grabbed two of the regular grenades. Both vehicles accelerated away from the gate and it started to close. From what he could see, the jeeps held Rija's men, but neither the general nor the secretary were in the vehicles. Too bad. If they had been, this night's work would have been much shorter.

When the jeeps were about twenty yards from the gate, the first of the disks exploded inside the compound. Everyone in the jeeps jerked around to see what had happened, but the drivers, after looking back, just kept going, slowing only slightly.

The second explosion went off inside the compound just as the jeeps were within twenty yards of Bolan's position. This time both slowed. The gunners in both vehicles had their rifles up and were looking back at the now-closed gate and compound walls. The guards on the walls were staring inside.

"Sitting ducks," Bolan said to himself softly as he tossed a grenade into each jeep as it went past.

One soldier glanced down at his feet as the grenade hit him in the leg and bounced onto the floor, but he didn't have time to react.

The first vehicle exploded into a ball of flame and flying body parts, and a moment later, the second jeep did the same, swerving as it did and hitting the ditch, setting off one of the traps in the ditch, as well.

The Executioner faded back into the jungle and headed around the compound walls, looking for any of Rija's escape hatches. He'd just kicked the proverbial anthill. Now the key was to get inside without being bitten.

21

Bolan found Imrich and Gabriel less than ten minutes later. Clearly the grenades had set off a few smoldering fires inside the compound—they could smell and see the smoke rising over the walls. Angry, shouting voices were plainly audible.

"Kicked them in the knee I see," Imrich said to Bolan, smiling as he appeared silently beside them, startling Gabriel.

"I was aiming a little higher," he said. "Any luck?" He hadn't seen anything on that side of the compound that even hinted at an emergency exit. More than likely the mouth of a tunnel could easily be hidden, but he didn't spot one on first pass.

Imrich nodded. "Caves. Tucked up against the ridgeline. It's where all the bats swarming the jungle come from, I'm sure, considering the amount of droppings around the mouth of the cave we found."

"Makes sense that Rija would pick a location over a large bunch of caves," Bolan said. "I wondered why he had picked this exact spot, now we know. It makes perfect sense that a fort this size would have siege tunnels."

"I'm betting that all his storage and half his control centers are underground," Imrich said. "And since he really didn't believe I would join him, he didn't show me that part of the operation."

Bolan knew that Imrich was right on the money. It made

sense that the kind of force that Hal Brognola described Rija as having would be larger than it initially appeared on satellite, and two bunkhouses just didn't seem like enough room to house an army large enough to take over the entire country. But if there were caverns under the compound, then the location and the storage capacity made a lot more sense.

Also, with most of the operation located in a cavern, any chance of a bombing run on the exposed part of the compound wouldn't take them out. It was all making more sense now.

"So there are some major entrances to the caves somewhere," Bolan said. "Large enough to drive trucks through." He looked at Gabriel. "Anything like that you might know about out here?"

"This entire area is filled with caves," Gabriel said. "Many are uncharted. Young children exploring in the caves sometimes never return. This is a dangerous area for such things."

"So, any sign of humans around the entrance you found?"

"None," Imrich stated. "But there wouldn't be if it's an emergency exit. And with all the bats, it would seem logical."

"Got any better ideas?" he asked.

Imrich shook her head and glanced in the general direction of the walls where the orange smoke of a fire still burned. "Those walls are sure death, and that just doesn't sound like much fun."

"I agree," Gabriel said.

"Agreed," Bolan added.

He scanned the area and pulled up a satellite image on his 3D map. The fort was in a protected position, but any position that was difficult to get into was also difficult to get out of. He looked at the area of the caves and came up with a plan.

"If the walls are a suicide run and he'll escape anyway, what if we just cut off the escape?"

"Isn't that what we're saying?" Imrich asked.

"Yes, but *we're* not going to block the escape…I am. The odds of all three of us avoiding all of the booby traps and security are slim, but if I can get by them and get into the tunnels I can start to drive them the other way and you two can help catch them in the middle."

"It's suicide to go alone," Imrich said.

"It's not great odds either way, but at least this plan has legs."

The woman glanced at the ground and then pulled two more guns from her pack and began to reload. She glanced up at Bolan. "Well, what are you waiting for? At least while you're getting your ass shot off we can try and get the secretary."

Bolan grabbed his gear, nodded and turned to head for the caves. Imrich appeared in front of him waving her gun in the air. "That's it?"

"You told me to go."

"Men are so stupid."

She pulled him forward and pressed her lips against his. Bolan wrapped his forearm around her neck and pulled her in closer, not bothering to put away his gun, either.

Finally, she stepped back with a smile. "At least try not to need rescuing, Cooper. I hate caves and have no desire to traipse in there after you."

Bolan watched as she rushed back to Gabriel, already giving instructions about their approach. He watched for a moment as she pulled apart the gear and couldn't help but grin as he moved to the caves. One thing about, Dusana, she always made a mission interesting.

Bolan slipped through the jungle and paused when he reached a small copse of trees outside the range of the cameras. He rifled through his bag for his earpiece and slipped it into his ear before turning on the phone. With this new device there were things he didn't quite understand, but the great thing about new technology was that it was willing to explain itself to you. He opened the wireless connection and booted the tactical software.

"Welcome to your Shadow 4 Tactical System. Operation?"

"Yes," Bolan said.

"Satellite, target painting and infrared enabled. Attach laser sight to weapon."

Bolan pulled out the small red laser sight and attached one to his Desert Eagle and another to his rifle. He lifted the rifle and stared down the open scope as the red pointer moved across the jungle foliage.

"Would you like to begin a tutorial?"

"No."

He grabbed two pieces of string and wrapped the display to the inside of his left forearm. As he started forward slowly, the small blips of infrared targets continued along their same paths. The first two sets of trip wires were easy to spot as he kept to edge of the tree line.

"Infrared field detected five meters ahead."

"What does that mean?" Bolan asked his chatty computer.

"Infrared fields are often an early warning system or can indicate an imminent threat."

"Well, I know that. I was just wondering which direction and the source."

"Field in four meters due east."

"What would be really helpful is if you told me the source," Bolan snarled. He was surprised when the computer answered back.

"Source is five meters east."

"Show me."

The 3D image showed the direction light from the stand of trees to his right. While the field might be technically four to five meters away, the first bomb location was only three and he moved around it to avoid being either blown up or picked up by the sensor.

Bolan moved to the mouth of the cave. From a distance, the cave appeared to be natural, but on approach he could see supporting beams and a dim set of lights guiding the way into the lower area. He cautiously stepped into the cave and his attention was arrested by high-pitched squeaking. Bolan cautiously raised his light to investigate the noise. The cave walls were moist and streaked with the dark silvers, blacks and reds of the different kinds of minerals that ran through the stone. As his light traveled higher, the first flutters of bats held little interest until Bolan realized that the dark patches that continued to lead down the corridor were throngs of bats huddled together, back from their nightly routine of searching for food.

He looked more closely. Thousands of bats.

The cave took a sharp turn and opened into a giant cavern. The cavern, roughly the size of a football field, was bustling with activity.

"Heat signatures detected," the device chimed in his ear.

"You just figuring that out?"

"Would you like advance notification of heat signatures?"

Bolan gritted his teeth. "Yes…" Sometimes, technology wasn't all that helpful, and this appeared to be one of those times.

Bolan scanned the red dots on his screen and saw a higher concentration to one side of the cavern. He peeked around the corner and watched as men moved through the cave and up the access stairwell. One guard, obviously bored with watching the back door, meandered along his posted route, his eyes rarely glancing back at his purported post and more thoroughly engaged with the actions of his comrades farther up the dreary corridor. Bolan tossed a rock in his direction. The clatter sounded booming to Bolan's ears, but the young guard was unfazed. Bolan tried again to get his attention by taking the butt of his rifle and tapping on the rock three solid times. The youth glanced back but dismissed the sound just as quickly.

Frustrated and sorry that a young man so obviously unprepared for this kind of battle might even encounter the Executioner, Bolan marched out of his hidden position behind the soldier and tapped him on the shoulder. Startled, the youth turned, his eyes widening in shock. Bolan's fist took him under the jaw, and he went out like the proverbial light. Bolan dragged the boy's collapsed form back out of sight and wrapped a zip tie around his wrists to help keep him away from the fight. Maybe, when he woke up, the youth would find a better way to make a living, but it was doubtful. In countries like Madagascar, Bolan knew, there were few jobs that offered the same security as militia work.

He consulted the figures on his phone. While one incompetent soldier protected the back door, the rest were in complete unison as they marched up the corridor. The section that appeared to be cells was constantly patrolled, and cameras in the corridor wouldn't make his task simple. But with time running out, simple would have to give way to last options. Bolan glanced behind himself and thought long and hard about his exit strategy, then returned his attention to the first tunnel.

For whatever reason, the bats nesting here were quite large, and while he didn't know the species, he suspected it was some kind of fruit bat, relatively harmless and usually found in jungle lowlands. Perhaps the shelter of the caves and the ready access to the jungle had led them here. Nonetheless, a bat with a three-foot wingspan would intimidate almost anyone. The fact was that when most people saw a bat, even a small one, something quite primitive took over and made them want to run for the hills. He anticipated that very large bats would produce a similar, if somewhat more spectacular, result.

Slinging his rifle, Bolan pulled two flares from the pack he was carrying. As he popped the flares, the tunnel filled with intense white light. The bats, mildly annoyed by his intrusion to begin with, began to stir. The sound of their squeaks and the odd, whispering noise of their wings got louder. He transferred the two flares to his left hand and pulled a small .38 out of the holster on his ankle. Taking quick aim, he began firing shots at the small lights lining the cave walls. The pop of the gun, followed immediately by the sharp *ping* of the exploding bulbs created the desired effect.

The noise and the continued flashes of light startled the bats out of their slumber. Screeching and flapping wings filled the main corridor and they flew in the opposite direction of the tunnel, seeking a different escape route—a route that sent them into the main cavern where they assumed Rija's soldiers were guarding the Secretary of State. Bolan came in behind them, enjoying the chaos as soldiers initially tried to fend off the large creatures but then quickly gave in to their more primitive urges.

Several screamed in outright terror, while others flailed their arms wildly in the air, dropping their weapons as they tried to fight off the bats. Confused, with nowhere to go, the bats circled, dived and continued to flail at the hapless soldiers. In the midst of this, Bolan slipped closer to what appeared to be some kind of small cell block.

Closing in, he saw that the bats hadn't done quite as much of his work as he'd hoped. Two soldiers stayed at their posts, white-faced, but still game. They watched as their comrades ran in all directions, ignoring the shouted orders of their superiors, using anything that came to hand—including their combat knives and even their guns—to swat at the bats.

In the confusion, sound wouldn't matter. He got within

range and pulled his Desert Eagle free. The closer guard turned just as he closed in, and Bolan aimed and fired without thought, putting a round into his target center mass. The guard fell over, dead before he hit the stone floor of the cavern.

The second guard heard the shot, spun and tried to bring his rifle to bear, but was too late and Bolan too close. The Desert Eagle boomed a second and third times. The guard staggered backward several steps, a stunned look on his face. He tried to raise his weapon one last time, but the strength was gone from his arms. He slowly slid to the ground, rolled onto his side and died.

Bolan turned to the small row of cells and observed that all of them were occupied. Most, it appeared, by locals who'd probably gotten on Rija's bad side or perhaps were militiamen who had disobeyed in some way. It didn't matter to him. He found the Secretary of State in the third cell he checked.

The lock on the door was metal, but it was old-fashioned. A bit of luck that Rija hadn't turned this area into a state-of-the-art facility, too. "Mr. Secretary," Bolan said, as the man's eyes widened and filled with hope. "Matt Cooper. I'm here to get you out."

"Thank God!" he cried. "I can't believe… Just…get me out of here!"

"Stand back," Bolan ordered, then turned the Desert Eagle on the lock. One round, placed perfectly, shattered the old metal and the lock fell to the ground with a soft clank. He yanked open the door, checking over his shoulder.

As he feared, the bats had finally started to fly back out the tunnel and the soldiers were calming down. Several were also looking their way, trying to determine what was going on.

"Mr. Secretary, are you injured?" he asked as the man stepped out of his cell. His clothes were filthy, but he didn't have any obvious injuries.

"No, but I'm exhausted, angry and I want to know what the hell—"

"No time for that, sir," Bolan interrupted. Three soldiers were headed their way and more would see what was happening any second. He handed his backup gun to the secretary. "Now we fight and we run."

"Fight and run?" Foster asked, still bewildered.

Bolan pointed at the soldiers. "That or death, sir, appear to be our only choices."

22

Sometimes politicians were the sort who seemed to have been born in a suit and tie, while others earned their stripes from serving in the military and working for a living. Thankfully, the secretary was in the latter group. He took the gun and managed to chamber a round before nodding.

Bolan reached out, dialed the safety to off, tipped the gun away from Foster, and then turned to face the oncoming horde, firing several quick rounds to force them to scatter and ensuring that the chaos lasted a bit longer.

The tunnels were wide, but the entrances still prevented everyone from descending at once. Bolan took aim and fired as the closest of the three men stuck his head out. The round took him in the forehead, spattering blood, bone and brains on the man behind him. It was an unpleasant sensation and distracted him long enough for Bolan to take the second man with a well-placed round in the throat. The third man had managed to wipe the gore from his face and was bringing his weapon to bear when three quick shots from the .38 sounded behind Bolan. He turned and saw the secretary already looking away, moving to free the other prisoners.

"Mr. Secretary, we don't really have time for that," he said. "The clock is ticking and I need to get you out of here."

"Make time, Mr. Cooper."

"All right, then," he said, knowing that to argue would take even longer. Somewhere above, Imrich and Gabriel would be doing everything they could to break through the front gate and cause chaos in the main level. "Cover my back."

Bolan reloaded and waved the prisoners back from their cell doors. The Desert Eagle turned the old-fashioned locks into so much rubbish as the doors swung open and the prisoners charged into the fray.

"Thank you," one man said, stopping to shake the hand of the secretary.

"Run" was his only reply. "Get out while you can."

Bolan began to lay down covering fire for the escapees. The prisoners grabbed weapons off of the dead and quickly became a force to be reckoned with on their own. Bolan grabbed the secretary and pulled him along the edge of the cave wall, looking for an opportunity to break through the lines and into the main compound. Two large explosions from the outside had men running back to the rear of the cave.

"Friends of yours?" he asked. Then paused, and added, "I hope."

"Yes," Bolan said shortly, scanning the area for a likely path going up.

"Good friends?"

"The best kind of friends," Bolan said.

"What kind is that?"

"The kind that come armed."

Bolan waited for the next wave to begin to move past them and then broke from their cover. He still needed to get the secretary out and find Rija. The man was a menace to the people, and he needed to die.

Spotting a narrow path between two large pillars of stone, he guided the secretary in that direction. The darkness, however, hid two more experienced guards who turned at their approach and raised their weapons. Bolan and the secretary fired at the same time, and both men went down in a heap.

"That looks like our way out," Bolan said.

"I think it goes up to the main compound," the secretary replied. "I've seen men going this way and not coming back through the cavern."

They moved forward, and the secretary grinned as the path widened and brighter lights ascended a steep ramp ahead of them. The victory, however, was short-lived as two bullets whizzed between him and Bolan, embedding in the soft stone of the cave wall behind them.

"Get down," Bolan snapped, shoving the secretary out of the way, and turning to see several more men headed in their direction.

The secretary positioned himself behind an outcropping, which wasn't much cover, but more than Bolan had. In mock surrender, he raised his hands, surreptitiously pulling the last small grenade from the pouch at his waist. The soldiers hesitated at his apparent surrender, which gave him the seconds he needed to pull the pin with his thumb. They got closer, keeping their weapons on him.

"When I say so," he whispered, "run."

The secretary looked as if he was about to argue, but then he spotted the dark mini-grenade in Bolan's hand and nodded. "Don't get yourself killed for me, Mr. Cooper."

"I don't intend to," Bolan said. He raised his arms higher as the three soldiers closed in. "Don't shoot!" he called.

Two of them started to lower their weapons, and Bolan released the lever on the grenade and dropped it at his feet. The incline of the ramp rolled it directly at the the soldiers. "Run!" he called.

Both the soldiers and the secretary took his advice, heading in opposite directions. Bolan yanked the assault rifle off his shoulder and opened fire, taking one soldier high in the shoulder and sending him stumbling to his knees. Backing up, Bolan fired one more burst, then turned and ran as the grenade exploded behind him.

The sound was tremendous in the confined space and sent sharp shards of rock buzzing through the air. Several clipped him, and one scored a long scratch down his cheek, drawing blood. It was possible his ears might never stop ringing, but there was no time to worry about such things. Ahead of him, the secretary continued moving, and Bolan picked up the pace, wanting to stay close. The secretary was obviously comfortable with a weapon, but he was hardly a soldier, let alone the kind of man with the training to handle whatever they might find when they reached the main level.

The ramp curved around to the right, then came to a halt in front of a large, metal door. A keypad with a card scanner was to the right. It was the same setup he'd seen on the door at the main compound. Bolan got close and handed his rifle over to the secretary. "Cover our backs and shoot anyone that comes up that ramp," he said.

"I understand," the secretary said, between shuddery breaths. "I'm a little out of shape for this sort of thing."

Bolan pulled his phone free of its case and extended the card that would let him hack the lock. "It's not a jog across the National Mall, that's for sure," he said as the card went to work.

The sounds of cautiously approaching men came from the bottom of the ramp. They were taking no chances this time. "Do you have another grenade?" the secretary asked.

"Fresh out," Bolan replied. "Just open up and lay down some covering fire."

Doing as he'd been told, the secretary squeezed several three-round bursts from the rifle. Bolan watched as the phone did its work, and a minute later the light indicating the door lock turned green. "Time to go," he said, yanking on the heavy handle. "Be ready."

"Hopefully, we'll find your friends on the other side of the door," Foster replied, backing up and firing one last burst down the ramp.

"I'm not taking that bet on this Murphy mission," Bolan replied as he opened the door and stepped through into a dark hallway. The secretary followed him and Bolan quickly slammed the door shut. It auto-locked, then he took his rifle back and used the butt of it to smash the control panel. No one was leaving this way or coming through for a while, anyway. He listened carefully and found that the compound was eerily quiet.

Something was wrong.

"Let's go," he said, moving down the hall.

"Where are your friends?"

Bolan shook his head. "I don't know, but I think we're going to find out."

IMRICH WAITED FOR Bolan to leave and then paused, considering her equipment, her current partner and the odds stacked against them.

"Are you thinking that we should leave?" Gabriel asked.

"No, though any sane person would. We need to find a way to get in there."

"Well, I think there might be a way," Gabriel stated.

"How? What are you talking about?"

"I saw one of their trucks tucked away."

"Where?" Imrich asked.

"About a quarter mile back. There was some camo set up around it. I think it must have been a guard post at some point."

"You might have mentioned it at the time," she snapped before realizing that he wasn't a soldier. It wouldn't have crossed his mind to think of a truck as a weapon. Imrich spun at the sound of gunshots. Several large bats flew out of the compound and she could hear yelling inside.

"Show me," she said. "Cooper just started his assault."

They double-timed back to the truck that Gabriel had seen. It was an old army deuce-and-a-half troop carrier. Imrich jumped into the cab and pumped the gas before trying to start the engine.

"It hasn't been here too long, the battery is still alive," she said as the engine started up.

"What do you think the odds are that this is up-to-date with their fancy horn system?" Gabriel asked.

Imrich peeked under the steering column and saw none of the tracking ware that she would have installed on the vehicles coming in and out of the compound.

"I don't think this one has it, but that's fine. I have another plan for this beast."

She grabbed four blocks of C-4 and strapped them to the grille of the truck then attached a small trigger to the bomb. Imrich grabbed a remote detonator from her pack and got behind the wheel. Gabriel slowly climbed in on the other side.

"You ready for this?" she asked.

"Just as long as your plan does not include us being suicide bombers."

"No suicide, but I did set the detonator on the C-4 just in case something happens and we don't make it through the gate ourselves."

They started the truck down the road toward the main gate. Imrich stomped on the gas and then wedged a stick against the gas pedal to hold it down.

"You ready?"

Gabriel didn't wait for her signal, but took the bullets that were heading in their direction as his cue to get out of harm's way. Imrich jumped next and rolled as she hit the ground, taking out a large, prehistoric-size fern along the way. The truck continued on its path, bullets from the fort filling the sides of the truck and one finding its way to the grille. Just as the vehicle struck the gate, it exploded, turning into an inferno as the C-4 detonated. The men guarding the gate screamed in agony as burning shards of metal rained down on them, and one staggered past the truck, a human torch who was dead and just didn't know it yet.

Imrich and Gabriel rushed forward, dodging the flames as they made their way through the gate. Two guards were standing watch. Imrich dropped into a roll, firing off a shot as she went. Gabriel wasn't as athletic, but he managed to land a bullet in the other soldier, slowing him down. Imrich turned and finished the job.

They were moving forward into the lower portion of the compound when they were stopped by a hail of bullets. Imrich looked up to see Rija standing on the central balcony overlooking the courtyard. In each guard tower, one of his personal bodyguards held a fully automatic rifle, trained on them both. She knew these men—and they wouldn't miss.

"Rija," she said. "I thought you'd be waiting."

"Dusana, I have missed the pleasure of your company while you worked with the American to undo all of our plans."

"They weren't *our* plans. All of this—this was your plan."

"Fair enough," he said. "But the damage is done. Most of my men are dead or running away, and the hidden cavern below is in chaos."

"Go ahead and kill us," she said. "That's what you're planning anyway, right?"

Rija chuckled and moved down from the balcony into the courtyard. He stayed far enough away that she couldn't get to him before one of his men took her down.

"Kill you?" he asked, still chuckling. Then he shook his head. "In time, perhaps, yes. But not until I've taken my pleasure from you—and my men have taken their pleasure from you. Many, many times, I think."

The distant sound of a door slamming caught his attention, and he nodded. "But first, there is the matter of your friend, Mr. Cooper. He will have to die, I'm afraid, and you're my best chance to arrange for that."

"I suppose you'll kill the secretary, too?" Gabriel asked, speaking for the first time.

Rija's attention flickered to him, then dismissed him as essentially a noncombatant. "Unless the U.S. gives me what I want, he'll die. Too many games, too much subterfuge. I'm tired of waiting and hiding. I will be the new government of Madagascar."

"That seems a bit overly ambitious at this point," Cooper's voice called from the edge of the courtyard. "Especially for a man who's about to die."

"I THOUGHT THAT WOULD be you joining us, Mr. Cooper," Rija said, still calm. "Why don't you join your friends out here in the courtyard? There's little point in continuing this fight."

Bolan stepped easily into the open area. "I agree," he said, gesturing toward the men in the guard towers. "Tell them to throw down their guns, and I won't kill them when I kill you."

Rija laughed. "You do not lack for bravery," he said. "I appreciate that quality." Then his eyes burned and his voice turned serious. "But enough of this. All of you will throw down your weapons and surrender, or my men will shoot you dead."

"Stand firm," Bolan told Imrich as she looked at him.

Rija noticed and said, "Where's Secretary Foster, Mr. Cooper?"

Bolan shrugged. "Dead. Down in the cavern below." He peered around once more. "Like most of your men."

"I don't believe you," Rija said. Turning to the guard in the far tower he called, "Go find him!"

The guard turned away from the scene below, which was exactly what Bolan had been waiting for. He pulled the Desert Eagle, spun toward the other guard, while Imrich, a split second behind him, raised her own weapon. They fired at almost the same moment.

The guard watching them was blown off his perch and hit the cobblestones of the courtyard with a sickening thud. Imrich's shot, however, was less accurate. She hit Rija in the knee. He screamed and fell.

Above them, in the tower, the guard turned back to see what was happening, which was when the U.S. Secretary of State shot him in the back of the head, killing him instantly.

Foster stepped out onto the balcony and gave Bolan a quick wave.

"Well done, sir," Bolan called. "Come down and join us."

At their feet, Rija squirmed in agony. Imrich's bullet had blown the knee completely apart.

"That was a lousy shot," Bolan observed. "Really bad."

"I *was* aiming a little higher," she said. "Sometimes, I miss."

Gabriel let out a long-held breath and said, "Is it over?"

"Almost," Imrich replied. She turned to Bolan. "He'll have a sat phone in his office, Cooper, which is probably up there somewhere." She pointed at the second floor.

"I'll go make a call, then," Bolan said. "And leave you to it." He took Gabriel by the shoulder. "Why don't you come along with me?"

"Why?" the cabbie asked. "Where are we going? What's Dusana doing?" Bolan guided him toward the stairs and the secretary joined them.

"What's she going to do to him?" the secretary asked.

"It's better not to think about it," the Executioner said. "Her kind of justice isn't very pretty."

Gabriel swallowed whatever words were on the tip of his tongue and opened the door to the office. They stepped inside, and Bolan gestured toward the heavy-duty satellite phone sitting on the desk.

"I think it's time to call home, Mr. Secretary," he said.

He nodded and picked up the phone. Bolan checked his. No satellite signal here, so he'd have to call Hal Brognola from the other phone. Not that it mattered. The secretary would see to it that the President called off the strike team, and they'd switch ops and become an extraction unit instead.

By sunrise, there'd be stealth choppers flying inland to pick them up and take them out of here. He wondered if Imrich would leave Madagascar or stick around, but he thought she'd stay. This was her home now.

The Executioner still had work to do, and Bolan knew that if he passed this way again and needed her help, Imrich would give all that she could. For Bolan, that would be enough.

* * * * *

TAKE 'EM FREE
2 action-packed novels plus a mystery bonus

NO RISK

NO OBLIGATION TO BUY

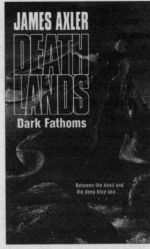

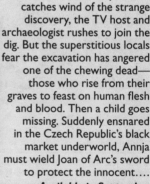

ROGUE Angel™

AleX Archer
BLOOD CURSED

A local superstition or one of history's monsters come to life?

Deep in the Bavarian forest, archaeologists unearth a medieval human skull with a brick stuffed in its mouth. When Annja Creed catches wind of the strange discovery, the TV host and archaeologist rushes to join the dig. But the superstitious locals fear the excavation has angered one of the chewing dead— those who rise from their graves to feast on human flesh and blood. Then a child goes missing. Suddenly ensnared in the Czech Republic's black market underworld, Annja must wield Joan of Arc's sword to protect the innocent....

Available in September wherever books are sold.

ROGUE Angel
AleX Archer
BLOOD CURSED

When a thirst for blood
signals certain death....

GOLD EAGLE®

GRA44